"Who are you trying to punish?"

Eduard's words were taunting as he let her go. "Me, or yourself?"

"I hate you!" she said, outraged.

"What for? For waking you out of the dream into which you fell when Powers touched you? Did you really think his kisses so unique that you'd never respond to any other man— even to me?"

"You forced that kiss upon me!"

"And you liked it! You don't even know yourself, Ruan Perry—let alone what makes a man. You don't want someone who bends the knee being gallant and tragic. You won't admit it, but the kiss taken is sometimes a lot sweeter than the kiss given. Who wants it to be tame and gift wrapped? No real woman, and certainly no man with a bit of vitality in him. And there's a dream I have...."

VIOLET WINSPEAR
is also the author of these

Harlequin Presents

and these

Harlequin Romances

Many of these titles are available at your local bookseller.

For a free catalogue listing all available Harlequin Romances and Harlequin Presents, send your name and address to:

HARLEQUIN READER SERVICE
1440 South Priest Drive, Tempe, AZ 85281
Canadian address: Stratford, Ontario N5A 6W2

VIOLET WINSPEAR

the château of st. avrell

Harlequin Books

TORONTO · LONDON · LOS ANGELES · AMSTERDAM
SYDNEY · HAMBURG · PARIS · STOCKHOLM · ATHENS · TOKYO

Harlequin Presents edition published November 1974
ISBN 0-373-15042-3
Second printing September 1977
Third printing October 1977
Fourth printing March 1979
Fifth printing May 1982

Original hardcover edition published in 1970
by Mills & Boon Limited

Part One

CHAPTER ONE

IT was all Taffy's fault – he ran into the theatre through an open side door and Ruan had to chase after him. She called urgently to him to come back, but the poodle ran on, his ears flapping like two small flags and his stump of a tail wagging. Taffy had a dash of the adventurer in him, and Ruan could have skinned him as he darted past some blocks of scenery and scampered right across the vast auditorium, giving a bark as from the stage a voice rang out:

> *Angels and ministers of grace defend us!*
> *Be thou a spirit of health or goblin . . . ?*

There the wonderful voice broke off, and as Ruan stepped over some cables she came in sight of the stage and saw a tall figure peering down at the bundle of curly fur who had dared to interrupt a rehearsal of *Hamlet* in this famous theatre.

'I'll be blessed, it's a poodle!' a woman laughed, but Ruan's eyes were fixed on the actor who wore a black sweater to his throat and narrow black trousers that made his legs seem even longer as he came with a supple stride to the edge of the stage and fixed his eyes not upon the little dog but upon Ruan.

His gaze passed over her, whimsical and startling. His eyes held hers, a smoky grey in his lean face with its chiselled cheekbones. She felt instantly the grace, the power, the spell of the born actor, and a secret shiver ran all through her. She knew he was Tarquin Powers, and yet there was something very human about his ruffled dark hair and the way he suddenly knelt on one knee to look down at her.

'Your pet, I presume?'

'My stepsister's.' Shy of those quizzical grey eyes, Ruan

bent down and tucked the truant poodle under her arm. 'Taffy likes to be let off the lead when we reach the grass verge of the river, and he's inquisitive about half-open doors.'

'Aren't we all?' murmured the actor in his deep, exciting voice. 'I imagine the stage-doorkeeper was picking a winner for the three-thirty and he didn't notice you. The pair of you are breaking one of the rules laid down by actors at rehearsal . . . no visitors.'

'I – I'm dreadfully sorry!'

'Don't be in too much dread.' His smile was a thing of magic, and for the space of a second her heart seemed to stop beating. It was almost unbelievable that she was talking to the star whom a few nights ago she had seen in a drama from a seat in the stalls. Her stepfather always had a box booked for the season, but Ruan loved the theatre for the acting, not as a place where it was the smart thing to attend when a famous company were in residence.

'You were tremendous the other evening, Mr. Powers. I saw you in *Othello* and loved every minute of it.' She smiled shyly at him, while Taffy wriggled in her arms and there was a restless stirring among the other members of the rehearsal.

'We must continue, *tovarish*.' A tall woman with a mannish haircut and a strong voice stepped forward. 'Tell the *matushka* to run along home and not play around the stage door again.'

Ruan felt everyone looking at her, amused as if by a child. She certainly wasn't one, despite a wistful, pointed face, and a pair of eyes that held a rare innocence. Her hair was unruly because she had been chasing Taffy.

'Our director speaks and I must obey,' said Tarquin Powers, but there was a dancing light in his eyes and Ruan had the excited feeling that she shared a secret with him. He would have liked to come and stroll beside the Avon with her and the poodle. It was incredible that she should think so, and yet instinct told her that she was right. She saw in his eyes an intrigued look and it half frightened her. He

8

was the leading actor of the play season, who was said to intrigue all women because he eluded the most determined of them.

He glanced at the tall woman who had spoken to him, and Ruan saw a look of admiration sweep across her rugged features, making them feminine for a moment – Valentinova, the clever stage director who had fled from Russia some years previously. She had a brilliant reputation, and was also rumoured to be a tartar who could make actresses weep and actors curse.

Tarquin Powers seemed to have her at his mercy. 'I am going to say goodbye to the girl and her dog. We may never meet again, *radouchka*.'

'You are incorrigible!' Valentinova glowered at the other members of the cast, and a girl with lovely fair hair gave a laugh and reminded Ruan of her stepsister, Charme.

'I'll go now . . .' Ruan backed away from the stage, and in an instant the actor leapt down with athletic agility to join her. She was very aware of his height as he placed an arm around her and Taffy and swept them along the central aisle, out into the foyer, and across to the main doors that opened upon the green and the river. She blinked, for the theatre had been dimly lit but for the stage lights. Out here in the open the sun was shining and the scents of spring were in the air. The swans preened themselves on the water, and the great theatre towered above her and the man who on its stage could hold sway over the hearts and emotions of those who loved the works of Shakespeare, Shaw, and Ibsen.

'It's like a scene out of *Le Lac des Cygnes*,' he smiled. 'In a moment the swans will rise to dance for us.'

Ruan looked at him wonderingly, for no one in her family circle spoke as he did; none of her stepsister's friends had so light a touch with words, and the associates of her stepfather never spoke of anything but money.

'The river and the swans are lovely at this time of the year,' she said, and felt that she was very prosaic and dull compared to the people who awaited him in the theatre –

9

especially the pretty actress with the long fair hair.

'Many things are lovely, a tree, a tower, a face glimpsed in a crowd and never forgotten.' His eyes held hers again and his thick lashes made shadows around the brilliant grey irises. He studied her, and then he smiled and made her smile with him. 'A single dimple in your cheek, eh? Is it for pepper or spice?'

She was both amused and confused. No one had ever bothered to say such things to her – and this was Tarquin Powers saying them!

'Do I make you feel shy?' he asked quite seriously.

'You're a famous actor.' She let Taffy out of her arms and he went to the water's edge, where he peered inquisitively at the white swans. 'I'm sorry we interrupted your rehearsal of *Hamlet*.'

'Have you ever seen it performed?' He lounged with unstudied grace against the pale stone wall of the theatre, a Hamlet figure all in black, his smile tinged with a little whimsical sadness.

She nodded, and knew that she would see *his* Hamlet and love it for the special reason that he spoke to her, and teased her a little.

'Do you live here at Avendon-upon-Avon, or are you visiting?'

'I live here. It's a lovely place, and I'm very fond of it.'

'Yes.' He swept his gaze over all that could be seen from the theatre. 'If only, though, we could turn back time for an hour and see it as it was in the sixteenth century. Would you like that?'

'It happens, Mr. Powers, when people like yourself transform a stage and speak the words of Shakespeare.'

'Indeed it does.' His eyes took her in, lazily, from her russet hair to her casual red shoes. 'Have you ever wanted to be an actress?'

'Me?' she laughed. 'I have freckles, and I'm shy.'

'Lots of actors are basically shy, miss.'

'Really?' She looked at him large-eyed. 'You seem very self-assured to me.'

'Ah, but you haven't seen me without my mask,' he quipped.

She looked at him uncertainly. Was that face that held strength and sensitivity only a mask? Was that smile put on with an effort? Was that tinge of sadness a clue to the real Tarquin Powers?

'I ... I mustn't hold up your rehearsal any longer,' she said.

'Before you go you must tell me your name.' Before she could move he took her chin in his fingers and tipped her face to the sunlight. 'Strange eyes, the colour of *violette des sorciers*. A touch of the Celt, unless I'm very much mistaken?'

'M-my name is Ruan Perry.' Her heart was throbbing with an emotion she dared not give a name to, for he was close to her, this stranger, and he was more attractive than anyone she had ever dreamed of knowing.

'Pierrette,' he said at once. 'How could you be called anything else? I wonder, Pierrette, if we shall ever meet again, to speak like this of swans and towers? Do you think it possible?'

She thought it highly impossible, and now her heart throbbed a sad note. 'I shall see you in *Hamlet*,' she said quietly.

'Yes, come to see me in my mask, Pierrette.' He let her go, and even as she murmured good-bye he had gone back into the theatre and she was alone once more. She called to Taffy and he came meekly and let her fasten his lead. They had to cross a main road to reach the terrace where she lived with her stepsister and her stepfather. The big house managed by Charme with the help of a couple of efficient maids and a cook. The smart residence with a Jaguar in the drive, and a drawing-room large enough for the parties Charme loved to arrange.

In a week's time she would preside over another to celebrate her birthday – a masked ball which Stephen St. Cyr would pay for and which Charme would revel in.

As Ruan reached the pavement, with Taffy trotting

along beside her, she glanced back at the theatre and saw the glint of the river. They were real, and her conversation with Tarquin Powers had been real. She had actually met the man behind the passionately romantic figure of Othello, clad in desert robes, haunting her by his performance for days afterwards.

Strange, how one thought of actors as being different from other people. Only on the stage were they invulnerable, like gods. In reality they were beset by problems like everyone else; they had tiny fears to overcome, and even their crowded lives could be lonely. She was sure that in the handsome grey eyes of Tarquin Powers she had glimpsed a certain loneliness.

The St. Cyr house was situated in a road lined with golden laburnum and purple lilac trees. Their house was detached and quite large, with a halfmoon drive, and steps leading up to the polished front door. Fine lace curtains hung at the long windows, and an air of comfort and shiny smugness pervaded the whole place. Ruan never felt at home here. Not even when her mother had been alive had she been able to feel settled in surroundings so stylized; so much the symbols of a successful Jones keeping up with all the other Joneses of Melisande Terrace.

Just as Ruan mounted the steps and sought her key in the pocket of her short, full skirt, a low-slung car turned into the drive and there was a swish of wheels on gravel as it came to a halt. Ruan watched from the top step as a young man leapt out and opened the passenger door beside Charme St. Cyr. She emerged with an elegant display of long silken legs, and the smile she gave him was the one especially reserved for good-looking males.

'Are you coming in for a drink, Simon, after being so nice as to take me shopping?'

'I'd like nothing better, honey, but I have to show up at the factory for an hour or Dad will disown me.'

Charme laughed, a gay and golden sound that matched her looks. 'Then I'll see you at the Castles' dinner-party this evening?'

'I'll pick you up, Charme.' He took her hand and a tiny smile quirked on Ruan's lips as this lanky young play-boy acted the gallant and kissed the elegant hand of her stepsister. Charme was without doubt the reigning beauty of Avendon, and her golden leopard-skin coat was more symbolic of her nature than Simon Fox ever dreamed. He slid into the car, waved and flashed off into the sunlight. Charme came slowly up the steps towards Ruan, and the poodle gave a bark of welcome.

'Hullo, my pet.' It was to the dog that Charme spoke. There was a look of coolness in her gold-flecked hazel eyes as she glanced at Ruan and took in her untidy russet hair. 'You look about sixteen, Ru. Why don't you make some attempt to be more chic, then attractive creatures like Simon might take some notice of you.'

Ruan's smile held the subtle quality of a secret. What would be Charme's reaction if told that Tarquin Powers had talked to her and suggested that her eyes held a certain sorcery?

Ruan unlocked the door and Charme swept in ahead of her. The pale panelled walls of the hall, the carpet of sapphire blue and the tasteful modern prints were there to set off Charme's colouring, as was the Regency furnishing and wallpaper of the sitting-room. She dropped her parcels on to the damask sofa and strolled to the sideboard where she poured herself a drink. She slid the leopard coat off her shoulders and stood revealed in a dress of cool rose-coloured silk.

She didn't invite Ruan to join her in a drink, one of the many subtle hints that the younger girl was not truly welcome in this house.

'I know it's your afternoon off from the shop,' she said sharply, not bothering to waste her velvety tones on her stepsister, 'but you might remember that Father and I have a position to uphold in this town and the clothes you're wearing make you look like Orphan Annie. You earn a fair wage at the Antique Shoppe, and my father has al-

13

ways been very generous to you. I'm really going to insist, Ruan, that you smarten up and get your hair coiffured. My friends think you're a joke!'

'I'm glad I provide them with a little amusement,' Ruan said coolly. 'I've noticed how bored they look at times.'

'You impertinent little devil!' Charme looked at the younger girl with a real flash of hatred in her eyes. 'If it wasn't for my father's goodness of heart you'd be living in a lodging house!'

'I'm perfectly willing to move out,' Ruan tilted her chin. 'It's your father who is against the idea. Each time I've mentioned it, he's talked of my mother and how upset she'd be if she knew. He's afraid people will think he doesn't care about me ... as if they'd even notice! And my poor mother's been dead for five years.'

'It's proof of my father's generosity that he married your mother, and cared for her and her *love-child*.'

The words were like little whips and Ruan flinched from them, the weapon Charme had used ever since her discovery that Ruan's lovely Irish mother had loved unwisely, and had married Stephen St. Cyr almost out of desperation when Ruan was seven and there were already signs of the heart trouble that in the end had killed Catrina. She had been so gay and brave. St. Cyr had lost his head over her, a widower with a daughter three years older than Ruan. He had saved Catrina from the drudgery of working as a domestic, and for that Ruan was grateful to him. Because of the few years of ease and comfort he had given her mother, she was willing to live at the villa and bear with Charme's unfriendliness.

Charme couldn't understand someone who liked to be by herself – a Barrie creature of the woods and the river, quiet and self-contained, with no feverish need for the admiration of other people, especially men.

The stepsisters faced each other, and when Ruan's eyes didn't waver, Charme gave a shrug and finished off her drink. 'I hope you're going to make an effort to look attractive at my birthday *masque*. I've invited everyone who is anyone, and that includes an important business associate of Father's who is coming all the way from Cornwall. I should have liked him to stay here at the villa, but he's booked himself rooms at the Bard and Harp. A very determined man, from all accounts.'

Ruan wasn't really listening. The friends and acquaintances of the St. Cyrs were not her kind of people, and she lost the drift of what Charme was saying as she stood, half-turned to the window, and dwelt on her encounter with the grey-eyed actor who had wondered whimsically if they would ever meet again.

At that moment the telephone rang and she felt a sense of relief as her stepsister left the room to answer it. She could hear her voice in the hall, gay and charming again, as she spoke to someone called Mr. Talgarth. 'So you've arrived already? How nice! Yes, Avendon is an attractive little town, and without a doubt our theatre is very famous and attracts some of the best companies. Oh, I'm sure you would enjoy going ... Father has a box booked for the season and you must join us! Please come to dinner on Friday evening, and we'll go directly to the Mask Theatre afterwards. Yes, a Shakespearean production. Are you a fan of the Bard? But of course I am, Mr. Talgarth. Who isn't?'

A little smile quirked on Ruan's lip as she caught the drift of the conversation. She knew very well that Charme preferred the lighter type of play; the quick thrust and parry of a Coward or a Rattigan. She liked to sit decoratively in her father's box at the theatre, and her basic lack of response to the magic of the plays was a distraction Ruan couldn't bear. This was one of the reasons why she chose to sit in the stalls to watch, to enjoy, to become lost in a world she understood without any effort. It was as if the Celt in her was attuned to the mystery and the wonder of it. Avendon was congenial, and life with the St. Cyrs was bearable, because from April to September of every year this riverbank theatre was transformed into a world of escape for Ruan Perry.

She was on her way upstairs to her room when Charme called up to her: 'Will you be going out Friday evening?'

Ruan turned to gaze down at her stepsister, who was a picture of elegance in her deceptively simple dress. 'I have a seat for the Mask. I can eat at the Old Mill Loft if you'd like me to.'

'That would simplify matters, darling.' Charme could always switch on the charm when getting her own way. 'I've invited that Cornish friend of Father's to dine here, and as Simon Fox will be joining us, it will make a neat foursome.'

'Three men to one woman,' Ruan quipped, with that light touch of mischief that made Charme's eyes go narrow, like a pretty cat's.

'You would be in the way,' she said pointedly.

'A state of affairs I'm accustomed to.' Ruan continued on her way up the stairs. 'I'll make myself scarce and eat at the Mill. As it happens I'm looking forward to Friday evening.'

'For any particular reason?' Charme's laughter floated up the well of the staircase. 'Don't tell me you have a date?'

Charme's definition of a date was an arranged meeting with a young man about town who would take her to the smartest restaurant and then to a show or a party. She wouldn't understand the quiet pleasure it would give Ruan to watch Tarquin Powers on the stage and be content to have spoken a few words with him. Charme would scoff and rob the meeting of its magic. 'You must have embarrassed him,' she would say, 'crashing in on their rehearsal like a clumsy schoolgirl. What's he like? Usually these actors are far older off-stage, and not nearly as handsome as they look in make-up and a flattering costume.'

'Yes, I have a date,' she fibbed from the stairs, just for the satisfaction of seeing her stepsister look amazed and curious. Then before Charme could ask his name (she knew everyone in town) Ruan hastened away to her room, her small oasis of books, deep window seats, and a record-player.

She put on a Chopin nocturne and sat in a window seat to listen and to dream a little. She wasn't a girl given to wildly romantic longings, but as she touched her cheek and felt the dimple that had no companion in her other cheek, her smile grew wistful. 'For pepper or for spice?' he had asked.

Ruan had a busy day at the shop on Friday; the tourist season was beginning and people from home and abroad were beginning to flock to Warwickshire. They came not only for the plays and the actors they could see at Stratford, and at the historical Mask at Avendon, but the wonderful old castle drew them. Avendon lay between Stratford and the castle, so it had become a stopping place for lunch and a stroll round the town with its timbered houses and quaint shops. Americans were particularly fond of buying mementoes of their visit, and of taking pictures with their movie cameras. They brought colour and gaiety into Avendon, and as the antique shop was part of a restaurant, known as the Lemon House and famous for many years for its pastries, Ruan was entertained by their talk, and also kept busy selling them the English antiques that were quite genuine.

Avendon prided itself on being less commercial than Stratford, and it was a fact that the more discerning visitors came here and found not only an attractive town, but a high standard of performance at the theatre that carried over its portal a mask of tragedy looking left, and a mask of comedy looking to the right.

To the right lay the river, where plum trees dripped their blossom over the Weir Bridge. Ruan loved it just there, and was well acquainted with the shady path that led to the Old Mill Loft, where she often ate a solitary dinner and watched the water rushing by over the wheel that was part of the charm of the place.

The waiter led her to a table tucked into a window alcove, and she was deciding what to order when her eye was caught by a trio of people seated a few tables away from her. Her heartbeats quickened. There was no mistaking that dark head, held with assurance and something of pride. There was no other profile quite the same as that of Tarquin Powers, no one else would wear a mulberry velvet jacket with such an air of lazy distinction.

She was struck by seeing him; it was somehow fateful, and yet she knew that actors from the Mask came to the Mill to sample its oysters and lager. The tradition was as old as the legend of the Bard.

'Oh—' She found the waiter giving her a grin, as if amused by a young girl's worship of a famous actor; one who had joined the International Company for their eight weeks at Avendon, and who would afterwards make a film in Italy or Greece, or fly to New York for a play directed by one of the giants of Broadway. Like other famous actors he probably found it refreshing and a stimulant to escape from the world of starry glitter to the true theatre, based on the Avon, where he could learn again some of the lessons and disciplines lost in the modern theatre.

'He's sampling our oysters,' murmured the waiter. 'Not that they're like the ones we sold in the old days. Refrigerated, miss. That's why we can serve 'em out of season.'

The Mill was said to have been a favourite supper haunt of Ellen Terry and Irving, and Ruan smiled, far more understanding of tradition than the usual run of nineteen-year-olds.

'I'll have steak and chips, please,' she decided. 'With a glass of lager.'

'Yes, miss.' The waiter ambled away and Ruan was able, from her alcove, to gaze almost unseen at Tarquin Powers and the two people who dined with him. One of them was the girl of the theatre, who with her tilted nose and long amber eyes had the look of an impish cat. The other man at the table was showing her how to prise an oyster from its shell, and Tarquin Powers watched lazily, the cleft down his cheek indicating that he was amused, perhaps charmed by the pretty actress.

Ruan leaned her chin on her hand and wondered what it

felt like to be thought pretty and amusing by a man so favoured by the gods. A little sigh drifted from her lips; she felt sure in that moment that she was one of those destined to be a looker-on, an observer of the loves and dramas of other people.

Strange that she had never cared before; never sighed until lately for the unattainable.

The waiter brought her steak and chips, and a slim glass of lager, and she was eating when the actors arose to leave the Mill to prepare for their evening performance at the Mask. It was then that Tarquin Powers glanced towards the alcove in which Ruan was half hidden. It was then that their eyes met again, as if he had sensed her quiet, unassuming presence – a pierrot of a girl in a beret worn sideways, and a kid jacket with a collar of lambswool.

He was so tall, so dark, standing there. And he recognized her. A smile quirked on his lips and a couple of strides brought him to her table.

'It's Pierrette,' he said. 'The girl with the poodle!'

'Yes.' Her smile was shy; without Taffy to hold like a shield against this man she was helplessly exposed to his attraction, to the wonder that he should speak to her again, remember her.

'Eating all alone?' A black brow arched, as if he failed to understand why she was alone. He glanced at her glass of lager, and when he met her eyes again there was a tiny grave smile in them. 'Do you like your own company, Pierrette?' he asked.

'I'm used to it,' she replied, and hoped she didn't sound too sorry for herself. 'I mean, one's own company is better than feeling *de trop* among people who don't like or understand the same things.'

'Yes, I know what you mean,' he said.

She looked at him, and saw beyond his shoulder the couple he had dined with. 'Do hurry, Quin!' called out the girl, and she stared at Ruan with recognition, while her companion glanced at his wristwatch and muttered something.

'You'd better go or you'll be late on cue,' Ruan smiled brightly, and knew there would always be someone to call Tarquin Powers away from her.

'Are you booked for tonight's play?' he asked.

'Of course,' she said. 'I wouldn't want to miss you as Petruchio.'

'I hope you enjoy the knockabout.' His smile flashed. 'And now I'd better go or my stage Kate will start throwing things at me before the play begins! *Au'voir*, Pierrette.'

'Good-bye, Mr. Powers.'

He quirked an eyebrow, and then he strode off and a moment later he and his fellow actors had left the Mill, and Ruan felt the sudden loneliness of her own company. She drank her lager and finished her meal, then sat on a while gazing out of the window at the dusky garden where the old wheel turned and the sound of water rippled and ran.

Still she could see his face as he had stood beside her table, gallant enough to remember her. She could from memory have drawn his features, virile, and yet with the added appeal of the ascetic about his temple, jawline and lips. He was a subtle mixture, she thought. Maybe that was why he found time to speak to her; to look at her as if she intrigued him because she was so different from the people with whom he worked and took his leisure.

A little thrill ran through her. He was nice. There was kindness in him, and seeing him close to had not dispelled his fascination.

She paid her bill, and her eyes shone eagerly as she made her way to the theatre. It was agleam with lights that reflected in the river, and over the marquee shone the names of the actors appearing in tonight's production of *The Taming Of The Shrew*.

Excitement quickened in Ruan. As she hurried towards the foyer of the Mask she had the strangest sensation of walking towards her fate. She laughed low in her throat, a gamine figure in her beret and short kidskin jacket over a slim short skirt. Her legs were long and slender beneath the hem, and her feet were clad in her comfortable scarlet casuals. She was picking up the temperament of stage people, she thought. Seeing symbols in the water; portents in a word, or a glance.

People were emerging out of their cars, and out of the shadows, a stream of gaiety and talk heading for the theatre, some of them pausing to look at the pictures and posters outside the Mask. There was a huge one of Tarquin Powers, clad in the doublet and hose of Petruchio, with a gleam of the devil in his fine eyes.

'Isn't he attractive?' exclaimed a woman.

'H'm, devilish good actor,' grunted a male voice, as if this excused to some extent the gift of a striking face. 'Saw him in that revival of *Dear Brutus* at that modernized theatre in Shaftesbury Avenue. Liked it. Yes, enjoyed it nearly as much as Coward years ago in *The Constant Nymph*.'

Ruan listened and smiled and felt that warm sense of being among people who understood good acting and appreciated the people who gave pleasure on the stage. After all, it was supremely hard work. Actors, somehow, had to be stronger, more co-ordinated, and dedicated to their art. If they looked upon acting as just a means of getting rich, then they never ranked really high with playgoers, who sensed instinctively whom to idolize.

Ruan entered the brightly lit foyer, rather antique and exciting with its cupids and its gilt rosettes, its mirrors and little gold chairs set against the walls. To the right and left of the foyer rose the staircases that led to the dress-circle and the boxes, and Ruan had taken her ticket from her pocket and was making for the swing-doors that led into the auditorium when her gaze fell upon a group of people standing and talking near the right-hand staircase. She knew the silver-haired figure who gestured a lot, and the lanky young man who stood admiring Charme in her white dress with its fine tracery of golden leaves, matching the colour of her hair and the half-wrap of soft fur that she

carried over her arm. Ruan didn't recognize the man who
dominated the group by his height, his darkness, and the
formidable strength of his features. He wore his smart dress
suit with a bold assurance, and there was a gleam of onyx
at his cuff as he lifted his hand and drew upon a cheroot.
He must be the visitor from Cornwall, and even as this fact
registered, Ruan was aware that the group had noticed her
and that Talgarth was looking at her with vivid blue eyes . . .
like a Celtic twilight. They startled because they were so
in contrast to his black lashes and brows. Eyes that saw a
great deal . . . perhaps too much for the comfort of the
person he looked upon.

'Ruan!' It was her stepfather who spoke, and she caught
the note of irritation in his voice, saw his nostrils go thin
as he surveyed her in her gamine attire, about to enter the
theatre through the door that led to the stalls. He beckoned
and she couldn't do anything else but obey the command
of his thin hand. Stephen St. Cyr was a lean silvery grey-
hound of a man, whose look of fragility was as deceptive
as his daughter's spun-gold charm.

'Child,' St. Cyr caught at her hand and pulled her into
the group. There was a strange eagerness about the gesture,
though his eyes continued to flash their annoyance that she
should be dressed so indifferently. He was a man who set
great store by appearances. It gave him intense pleasure
that his daughter Charme was so good-looking and had
superb dress sense.

His thin fingers tightened on Ruan's as he turned to
smile at the man who towered above him, and Simon Fox.
Simon was looking at Charme and there was a smile about
his lips.

'Eduard, I'd like you to meet my other daughter,' St.
Cyr said fulsomely. 'This is the child I was telling you
about. Her dear mother was the loveliest Irish girl, and so
tragic really. I managed to make her happy for a few short
years, but in the end she faded like the wild flower she was.
Being a Celt yourself, Eduard, you no doubt believe in
destiny?'

22

'I believe without being devoted to the idea,' said Talgarth dryly. His eyes were upon Ruan, who was impatient to get away, to fly through those swing-doors that led to the stage, where at any moment the curtains would open upon Padua and the magic of the play.

'I am happy to know you, Miss Perry.' The voice was arresting, drawing Ruan's eyes to the rugged face, with a hint of great passion about the mouth. He reminded her of high stony cliffs, she thought, and she hovered beneath his glance and his strong shoulders like a moth on the edge of taking wing.

'I'm pleased to have met you, Mr. Talgarth.' She shook his hand hurriedly, cast a rather defiant glance at her stepfather, and then was darting away and calling back over her shoulder ... 'I don't want to miss anything. Perhaps I shall see you all after the play ...'

As she breezed through the swing-doors, she noticed that Talgarth took a pull at his cheroot with a look of total unconcern. 'Really!' said Charme, and Ruan knew that later on she would receive a severe scolding from her stepsister. It wasn't that she meant to be impolite, but she wasn't going to miss Tarquin Powers' entrance on stage for the sake of chatting with a friend of Charme's. They rarely noticed that she was alive, anyway.

She found her seat and waited expectantly for the curtain to rise. The auditorium was large and held quite a number of people, and again, as on the other evening she had been here, there was a sense of excitement and tension in the air, only palpable when playgoers anticipated a performance out of the ordinary.

Ruan was secretly thrilled by what she sensed in the atmosphere of the Mask. These rows of people in their red plush seats were tensed up to see Tarquin Powers, attuned to the magic that he possessed as an actor; a power that was also luminous, so that on stage he seemed at once very vital and yet of another world. He could be loved but never possessed. He was alone, and yet he knew the way to touch other people. He could beguile them, and he could hold

23

them at his mercy ... some critics had gone as far as to say that the ghost of Garrick lived in this twentieth-century actor who was only thirty-two; who was of Huguenot descent, and the son born late to Margo Powers, the poetess and clairvoyant.

As people whispered and the tenseness increased with each stirring of the crimson curtains that hung from the proscenium arch, with its Janus mask that wept and smiled at the same time, Ruan glanced up at one of the ornate theatre boxes to the right of the stage.

Charme and the three men had taken their seats, and Ruan noticed that the Cornish visitor to Avendon was looking around the theatre with a great deal of interest. Charme spoke to him, and he smiled briefly in return. He seemed a strange friend for the St. Cyrs to have, and Ruan supposed they had met him during that trip they had taken to Penzance a few weeks ago. Stephen St. Cyr was in business as a land and estate agent, and he travelled quite a bit. Often on his return from one of these trips he was all smiles and redolent of expensive cigar smoke. Around the beginning of the year he had been personally responsible for a sale of land running close to a million pounds. The commission had bought the small cabin-cruiser which he and Charme had gone to Cornwall to view.

Had they bought the boat off Eduard Talgarth? Somehow he had the look of a sailor. Men with penetrating blue eyes always reminded one of the sea.

Then it was that those blue eyes found her in the stalls of the theatre. They were like a stab of blue lightning, raking her face and recognizing her as the girl who had been impolite to him. He looked as if he wouldn't forget it in a hurry, and a little shiver ran through Ruan. She hoped she wouldn't run into him too often at the villa, or around Avendon. He seemed alien to the place; as if he belonged among rocks and the lash of high waves, and was dangerous to cross.

Ruan glanced at Charme, a cool and elegant picture in her expensive dress. Was her stepsister taken with the man?

If so, then it was a surprise to Ruan. Charme usually liked men she could order about, and Eduard Talgarth looked every inch his own master!

Her speculations went no further, for in that moment the music quickened from the orchestra pit, and there was a silken swish as the stage curtains opened and the theatre lights dimmed.

Ruan's heart beat fast. She forgot instantly the dark stranger in the box overhead. She saw only the stage, the scenery, the actors in their colourful costumes. She lived only for the moment when Tarquin Powers would make his appearance as Petruchio; a man apart, more handsome and vital than other men, and yet real to her because he had smiled at her, spoken to her, given her the name of Pierrette.

It hadn't been a dream that there had been a promise in his eyes of finding her again in Avendon.

But it didn't happen that night. After the last curtain call, after the warm applause had died away, the star was besieged at the stage door. Ruan lost sight of him in the crowd of fans, and with a smile she tucked her lambswool collar about her face and made her way home in a soft rain. In the drive of the house stood a black Lancia, evidently owned by the man she was out to avoid. She stole round to the kitchen entrance and luckily the door was not yet bolted and she had a key. She let herself in very quietly, drank a glass of milk ice cool from the fridge, then tiptoed past the lounge to the staircase.

She heard the rumble of a deep voice, caught the clink of coffee cups and the ripple of Charme's laughter.

Mr. Eduard Talgarth was indeed being made welcome at the villa! Ruan nibbled one of the cream crackers she was taking up to bed, and decided to be soundly asleep when Charme came upstairs. After the magic of seeing Tarquin Powers she didn't feel like being scolded over the stranger from Cornwall.

CHAPTER TWO

IT was the evening of Charme St. Cyr's birthday party and all was excitement at the house on Melisande Terrace. Coloured lights were strung out round the drive, and the members of a small orchestra had just arrived with their musical instruments. The buffet was laid in the lounge, where the drinks would also be served. The drawing-room had been denuded of its furniture and the floor prepared for dancing. The french doors were open to the garden, where more fairy lights were strung out round the trees, glimmering on the clusters of lilac and laburnum.

Charme was delighted that it was a fine evening, and enchanted with her costume, which was made in the style of an eighteenth-century court dress. Her mask, which she had just unwrapped, was a genuine antique with a jewelled handle ... a gift from the dark-browed, rather dangerous-looking new friend who had come all the way from Cornwall to attend the party. Each guest had been asked to come in fancy costume. Ruan had helped to send out most of the invitations, but a few more had been dispatched on Saturday and Charme had been rather mysterious about them.

Ruan raised the jewelled mask to her eyes and studied Charme through the openings. She wondered again where Eduard Talgarth fitted into Charme's plans. 'You look odd!' Her stepsister almost snatched the mask from her hand. 'Be a pet and take Taffy for a run. I've been so rushed off my feet I haven't had time to spare for him.'

Ruan found the poodle under the piano, barking at one of the members of the orchestra. 'That pooch is no lover of music,' growled the young man.

Ruan thought it diplomatic not to remark that Taffy adored Chopin and was also partial to Ivor Novello's music. She tucked him under her arm and was going out of the

26

front door as her stepfather entered.

'Where are you off to, Ruan?'

'Charme asked me to take Taffy for a run.'

'Is she excited?' Stephen St. Cyr broke into a fond smile. 'Well, don't be too long. The party begins at eight-thirty.'

She nodded. 'The fairy lights look nice.'

'Yes, child.' A lean hand fondled Taffy. 'Talgarth will be at the party, Ruan. I'd like you to be – friendly. He's rather a personage down there across the Tamar, and I was rather annoyed the other evening by the way you ran away from the chap. You mustn't be frightened of men, Ruan. You mustn't let your mother's mistake ... well, you understand what I mean. We don't want you to end up as a spinster,' he laughed, his eyes flicking the russet hair that hung straight to Ruan's shoulders, the same colour as her mother's had been. 'You aren't unattractive, you know. You have a certain elfin appeal that some men like.'

Ruan was struck a little sideways by this conversation. Her stepfather had never said before that she had any ornamental value. 'I promise not to clutter up any of your shelves, Stepfather,' she said lightly. 'I'll move out if I look like being in the way.'

'Ruan!' His pale-blue eyes took on a glitter. 'Now that's no way to talk to me. I have your best interests at heart.'

He didn't bully her quite as much as Charme, she admitted to herself. 'I'll give Taffy a run by the river and I'll hurry back to the party,' she promised.

He nodded, and she felt him watching her as she ran down the steps with Taffy bounding at her heels. Her stepfather was certainly keen on Eduard Talgarth being made welcome at the villa, which must mean that the Cornishman was well off and maybe a good prospect as a son-in-law. Charme wouldn't marry for love, in Ruan's estimation. She would place worldly considerations before romantic ones, having always given the impression that love itself was elemental and uncivilized.

Ruan strolled along beside the river and she couldn't help wondering what the dark Cornishman's views were on love . . . he looked, himself, rather elemental.

From across the river she could see the lighted theatre, and she hoped ardently that she might again have the good fortune to speak to Tarquin Powers. Right now he would be in his dressing-room preparing for *Arms And The Man*, in which he played the role of Sergius. Ruan would have loved to see him in the Shaw play, but she didn't dare play truant from Charme's party.

It was a little crazy of her to feel so romantically about a charming stranger, but she couldn't fight the magic of it. It was so thrilling that such a man should notice her, smile at her, and say a few kind words: It would be something to remember when he left Avendon . . . but right now she had become aware that a sports car had drawn into a nearby kerb, and that the driver was steadily watching her as she stood in the gloaming while Taffy chased a large moth. The man's face was in shadow, but Ruan felt the impact of his gaze.

And then to her dismay Taffy darted towards the parked car and she had to turn and call him. She saw the man fully then. He was leaning slightly forward, talking to Taffy, who was wagging his stumpy tail in friendly recognition.

Ruan's dismay increased, strangely enough, as she recognized that dark and vigorous Celtic face; that iron-dark hair, fitting close like a helmet. Her hair blew against her cheek as she looked at him, and she saw that Taffy was on the step of the car, up on his hind legs and fondling with his nose the lean hand of Eduard Talgarth.

'Good evening, Miss Perry,' he said. 'The Mask Theatre seems to have a fascination for you. Are you stage-struck?'

There was the trace of a smile on his lips, and it seemed to her that he mocked her.

'I bring Taffy here to have a run round the trees,' she said stiffly. 'Avendon is a town and it's a mile or so to the open country.'

'You should see Cornwall – Taffy would go delirious let loose on the moors. Miles of them, covered in heather high enough to hide a girl, let alone a poodle.'

28

'I'm afraid I shall never have the pleasure, Mr. Talgarth, of hiding myself in Cornish heather.'

'Who can tell what may happen, Ruan Perry, to make you want things you may never have dreamed of wanting? Life can play strange tricks on people, but you're too young to know about that.'

'I'm nineteen, and I've always known that life can be sad, Mr. Talgarth.'

He nodded, as if he remembered what St. Cyr had said about her mother. 'One finds compensations for the loss of something loved – is yours the theatre? You're fond of it, aren't you?'

'Yes.' She spoke shortly, for she didn't wish this conversation with a friend of Charme's to veer in any way towards Tarquin Powers. What a joke, what an amusing incident to laugh over! Funny little Ruan, all aglow because an actor threw her a smile and a few words ... crumbs from the banquet he probably shared with his lovely leading ladies.

'I must be getting home ... the party will have begun and I'm not even dressed for it!' She bent to fasten Taffy's lead, and as she did so Eduard Talgarth opened the car door and the poodle skipped inside and jumped on the spacious front seat. 'Really!' Ruan glanced up and met the dominating eyes that held hers as he pushed the door a little wider.

'You might as well jump in, child,' he said. 'I'm going to the party and we'll both get there a little quicker if you'll stop disliking me for five or ten minutes. Come on, force yourself!'

She flushed, and at any other time she would have marched off independently and left him to drive the poodle home. But it was growing late, and the habit of conciliating Charme was too strong to be ignored on her birthday. She slipped into the car and felt the give of the leather seat, the brush of Talgarth's arm as he closed the door. He started the Lancia and they swung out of the layby on to the road, and he headed in the direction of Melisande Terrace.

Taffy sat erect between the two of them, and the evening breeze felt cool against Ruan's cheeks. She half-turned to gaze back at the theatre, and then remembered the shrewd glint in Talgarth's eyes when he had asked if she was stage-struck. 'You aren't wearing fancy costume,' she said. 'Charme wanted everyone to come in masquerade—'

'I'm not the sort for dressing-up,' he drawled. 'Your sister will have to excuse me on the grounds that I'm from the wilds of Cornwall and that I don't go to many parties.'

'She'll make you wear a mask,' Ruan warned. 'We're all to be masked until the stroke of midnight.'

'I'll submit to being masked,' a smile creased his cheek. 'In any case most people wear a sort of "mask" a good deal of the time. It's rare to come across someone who is completely guileless.'

'If people weren't a little secretive,' said Ruan, 'then they'd be much less interesting.'

'Wise child!' He looked directly at her, a look that lasted but a second and yet left her with the vivid impression of a man who was very deep, and capable of many things ... including kidnap.

'You've driven past the terrace where I live!' she exclaimed.

'Ah, so I have.' Traffic was quiet along the High Street, so he backed the car and swung it expertly into Melisande Terrace, with its detached villas all looking rather alike until they came to the one with the fairylit drive and several cars already parked there. There was a sound of dance music. The party had begun.

'I'd better go in through the back way.' Ruan pressed the lever that opened the car door and as she slid from the seat she felt Eduard Talgarth's sea-blue eyes upon her. The wind had ruffled his hair and a dark strand was caught upon the peak of his left eyebrow; always raised in that slightly wicked way. A trace of a smile was on the lips that somehow belied the hard, cool authority of the rest of his face.

He wasn't a man who could be called handsome, but the

very strength of his features, that touch of the relentless, made him far from easy to forget. He was like the Cornish corsairs of long ago; the smugglers who brought brandy and laces from Brittany, to hide in the water-lashed caves that had stone passages leading to dark old mansions on the cliff tops.

Those dark, lawless seamen had to be part of the history of Talgarth, for he had sailed the oceans of the world himself, a skipper who had dealt in all sorts of wares, some of them exotic, some of them contraband. Charme had told her, 'He's retired from the sea to a house in Cornwall that used to belong in his family years ago. A strange place, they say, the people down in Penzance. A sort of French-styled house called the Chateau of St. Avrell. There was a French prince who fled from a rebellion. He was said to have built it for the French girl he hoped to marry. Eduard's mother came from Brittany.'

'What sort of costume are you wearing for the masquerade?' he asked dryly, as if he thought her a child who would enjoy disguise.

'You mustn't ask, Mr. Talgarth.' She was out of the car, and Taffy came reluctantly to her call. 'That's part of the fun, guessing who is who.'

'Perhaps I should have worn a scarlet scarf around my forehead.' His eyes taunted, as if he knew her thoughts of him. 'Would that have been appropriate?'

'Yes,' she said frankly. 'You would make a very good pirate.'

'They weren't good, Ruan Perry. They took what belonged to other people.'

She had a mental picture of Simon Fox, who had been courting her stepsister for almost a year, but it was really none of her business if this stranger came all the way from Cornwall with the intention of running off with Charme. When he saw her tonight in her court dress, he would want all the more to install her at the Chateau of St. Avrell. He was probably quite rich, and Charme's evaluation of herself was that she was beautiful enough, and charming enough, to rate a man of means.

'I must go in!' Ruan ran and Taffy chased at her heels.

By eleven-thirty the house was packed with people. They were dancing in a crush in the drawing-room, seated in couples up the staircase, eating sandwiches and cake off paper plates. Some were out in the garden, masked figures laughed among the trees. The party was an enormous success, and many of the costumes were inventive and amusing.

One man stood just inside the open french doors of the lounge. He wore a Hungarian tunic buttoned at the shoulder, narrow dark trousers and topboots. A red-lined cloak hung in dashing folds around his tall lean figure, and a mask of black velvet concealed most of his face.

Ruan couldn't take her eyes from him. She was at the buffet table, a sausage roll in one hand and a Coke in the other. She wore the costume of a pierrette, with her hair tucked under a peaked cap, and a silver mask across her eyes. A little halfmoon of silver was affixed to the dimple in her left cheek.

Slowly she took a bite from her sausage roll. She looked a shy little clown as she stood alone, and her heart began to beat fast as the cloaked figure moved and began to thread his way through the chattering groups of people to where she stood. He came to her, deliberately, inexorably, and she knew him with every nerve in her young body.

'I feel the same as you,' his voice was deep and warm above her head. 'Sausage rolls are irresistible.'

She knew that mobile hand, that bloodstone ring on the middle finger, the magic of his voice. As he took a roll and bit it in half, she broke into a smile.

'It's you!' she whispered, in a kind of wonder.

'At your service, Pierrette.' He gave her a gallant bow. 'Mmmm, excellent sausage rolls. I think I'll have another. Tackling Shaw's verbal acrobatics for a couple of hours always give me an appetite, and along with Ann Destry and her fiancé, and one or two others, I came straight from

32

the theatre without bothering to change. It said on the invitation cards that the party was to be in fancy costume, so here you see me – Sergius!'

The party for Ruan was suddenly lit up with stars and fanfares. She hadn't dreamed that her stepsister had invited Tarquin Powers and other members of the company to her birthday *masque*, and it was a wonderful surprise. Unintentional, of course, for Charme had no idea that the actor had struck up an acquaintance with Ruan.

'I'm sure you'd like something stronger than a Coke,' she said, and smiling, she led him round the table to where the bottles of wine, vodka and whisky stood in a rather depleted cluster. 'Help yourself, *tovarich*.'

He laughed and his eyes were upon her as he helped himself to vodka and tossed it back in the appropriate manner. 'I'd better not toss the glass in the fireplace, eh?'

She smiled and shook her head, and her eyes were held by his through the openings of his black velvet mask. 'I just live here,' she said, and then a gasp escaped her as he swept his arm around her waist and suggested that they dance. The drawing-room was packed and all they could do was shuffle about on the same spot. But that in itself was exciting. It meant that she was close to Tarquin, and she was thrilled, shocked, by her response to him. When he spoke to her, his lips close to her ear because of the din, she felt herself defenceless, at the mercy of something she should fight. He was Tarquin Powers, not a boy from Avendon, with whom it would be cosy and right to fall in love.

Love ... even as the word shook her heart, she caught Charme's eye and tried to look as if she hadn't a clue to the identity of her dashing partner. Charme was standing with her Cornish guest, who had permitted himself to be masked but who stood out like a rock in a garden in his sober dark evening suit. He looked directly at Ruan and she knew from the thoughtful raising of his left eyebrow that he recognized her partner. He had a seaman's eyes, penetrating even through a mask, and trained to see

33

further than other people. What did he see right now, a foolish young girl falling in love with a man she could never hope to hold?

'Let's get away from the crowd!' Tarquin danced her through the french doors, thrown wide open to let in the evening air. There was a narrow terrace and three steps to the garden, and his fingers held hers as they strolled down a path and came to a halt beneath a lilac tree, purple-flowered but with a grassy tang.

'It's a lovely spring night, Pierrette.' He drew aside a cluster of lilac so the new moon could shine through. 'Have you ever wanted to swing in the cradle of the moon, for it's there that a pierrot belongs, far above the crowd, a little sad and also rather charming.'

'I'm glad you like my costume, Mr. Powers.'

'You mustn't be formal with me, Pierrette'. His eyes laughed down into hers. 'You must call me Quin, which is what I prefer to be called when I step off the boards.'

The fair girl had called him Quin, and suddenly she remembered what he had said, that Ann Destry had come to the party with her fiancé. Lovely as she was, and Tarquin's stage lover, she had no place in his private life except as a friend!

'Would you very much mind,' Ruan crushed the lilac in nervous fingers, 'if I called you Tarquin? I ... I rather like the name.'

'You may call me whatever you like,' he said amusedly. 'The stage is littered with darlings and pets, and some women have been known to call me a brute.'

'Oh, but why?' Ruan couldn't believe that he could ever deserve such a name.

'For various reasons,' he said, a quirk of a smile on his lips. 'Romantic actors are supposed to be great flirts, on and off the stage.'

'And you are a flirt?'

'No, Ruan.' Now he spoke seriously, and his brilliant eyes held hers with their deep humour, their whimsicality, their love of the acting art itself. Suddenly a laughing

34

couple chased by them, ran around the tree and cut between them. Tarquin raised his hand and slipped his mask from his face; the moonlight was upon it and she saw that his fine features were rather tense.

'Let's get out of this madhouse,' he said. 'Where can we go?'

'Out through the side door ... it's only five minutes' walk to the river.'

'Then come on!'

'Can we go like this?' She was laughing a little as she removed her pierrot's cap and her hair tumbled about her face.

'Yes, why not?' He caught hold of her hand and they fled from Charme's party, leaving behind them the lights and the laughter; walking quickly away from the house, almost with urgency, as if there was so little time for them to be alone; only these brief pauses between their separate lives.

'You don't mind if I kidnap you?' He looked down at her as they paused at a kerb to let a car swish by. It had rained a little, but now the air was soft and cool and moonlit.

She shook her head, and thought briefly of that other man who looked capable of running off with a girl. Other girls, never Ruan, yet here she was at midnight, her hair streaming out behind her as Tarquin ran her across the road towards the silver-dark glint of the river. A lone white swan glided by like a ghost – a restless, lonely swan perhaps, who wasn't sleepy enough to join its mate on the little island where the birds slept.

Ruan shivered a little, with excitement more than cold, and Tarquin took off his cloak and draped it around her, and she didn't dare to meet his eyes. His hands as they touched her seemed like the hands of a lover, but it would be folly to let herself dream that he wanted more than a confidante, someone to talk to of swans and towers.

'There!' He clasped the cloak, and they walked beside the river and the theatre stood dark and silent across the water and they were the only disturbers of the peace. The lone swan made no sound, pale neck bent as it glided, a Pavlova of the moonlight.

'What does it feel like,' she asked, 'to walk out on a stage in front of a thousand people?'

'Terrifying,' he said at once. 'Always in those first few moments it's a kind of hell, like judgment day. Even the most seasoned actor is sure he will forget his lines, stumble over something, be out of accord with the mood of the playgoers. The intense relief when you begin to speak, the joy of it when you begin to feel those first ripples of warmth rising towards you from the auditorium – it's tangible, Ruan, like the salt in sea-air. An actor senses it with his nostrils, and then he knows with all his nerves that he has captured a thousand souls in the net of the play. It's a wonderful feeling then. You want nothing else. You touch the stars.'

'It's like Lawrence's description of love,' she smiled. ' "Splendour, pride, assumption, glory and lordship." '

'Exactly like that, Ruan.'

They paused to gaze across at the theatre, his world which she could only enter as a visitor, as a lover of the play. Yet when she looked at him in the moonlight, his profile outlined in all its clarity against the deep violet sky, she knew that she loved him beyond the play; from the moment she had heard him speak, touching her heart that yearned for something to love.

Their glances interlocked, and there was no more fighting what she felt for him. She knew she surrendered part of herself during that glance. Something tender – broodingly tender – stole into his expression.

'You aren't much like your sister,' he said.

'Well, we aren't really related. Her father married my mother, but apart from that we've very little in common.' Ruan smiled. 'Charme is considered the belle of Avendon, and though I admire her beauty, I'm afraid we don't get along all that well. It's a case of a stray kitten sharing the house with everyone's pet. Charme likes cushions and cream, but I'd be content with—' Ruan bit her lip, for she had been about to say affection. Since her mother had died she had not been loved, only cared for in a material sense.

Tarquin was listening carefully, and suddenly the floodgates opened and Ruan was telling him everything. 'I'm not really ungrateful to the St. Cyrs. Stephen was good to Catrina, my mother. I never knew my real father. All I know is that he was a soldier and Catrina loved him. She always said he meant to marry her, but suddenly he was posted abroad and the next thing she heard was that he had been killed. She was a maid in his mother's house and she didn't dare to tell anyone her secret. She ran away and for seven poor but happy years we were together, until she married my stepfather. Then while I was at boarding school she became ill and died . . . Tarquin, do you think I should feel ashamed because my parents weren't married? Charme thinks so. She finds me a bit of an embarrassment.'

'The showy things of life are often shallow, Ruan, holding but a candle to the sun.' Tarquin traced with his fingertips the fine bones of her face. 'A child of love is a thing of love, Pierrette. Like a goblet chased all over with rare, strange patterns. Filled to its brim with a warm wine. It's what we are, Ruan, what we make of ourselves that counts.'

And with those kindly words he made her feel that she could never again be hurt by her stepsister's remarks. It was strange, holding a dreamlike quality, that she was alone like this with the famous Tarquin Powers. She had the feeling that she answered some transient need in him; a reaching back into his youth, perhaps, for the innocence and trust he saw in her eyes.

'You should have been called Alice,' Charme had once said to her. 'You look one minute as if you're in wonderland, the next instant as if you're at the mad hatter's tea party.'

Ruan smiled to herself. Didn't Charme understand that there was a certain wonder, and a certain craziness to living?

'What are you smiling about?' A lean hand tilted her

face to the moonlight, so that it seemed to grow even more wistful.

A tremor ran through her, for she was unused to the touch of a mature and attractive man. 'I'm wondering if my stepsister noticed that we stole away from her party.'

'I hope she did,' he chuckled. 'It will teach her that glamour isn't everything, and that "Ruan" means "deep-running brook".'

Ruan's eyes widened with surprise. 'How did you know that?'

'I looked it up in a book,' he teased. 'As a matter of fact I used long ago to be taken on holiday to Cornwall, that most Celtic of kingdoms. There was a place where the rocks looked like knights at their vigil, where the moors made one think of the romantic stories of Camelot, and one large rock with a complete archway through it which led to a cave I called the Grail. I used to keep there my collection of sea-spoil – shells and pieces of quartz and hanks of seaweed.'

He paused and smiled, and his arm slipped around Ruan in a kind of careless camaraderie. 'I'm trying to remember the name of the place – what stands out in my memory is the house that stood way up on the cliffs. It was like a chateau, strangely enough, with turrets and a tangled garden. Nobody lived there, yet a notice on the gate said Trespassers Beware! I suppose that part of it intrigued me more than anything else. I trespassed and found the windows shuttered and ravens nesting on the roof. There wasn't even a caretaker. It was as if the place was haunted and no one dared to live there.'

Ruan caught her breath; for one wild moment she was tempted to tell him the name of the house, and of the man who now lived in it – unafraid of ghosts. Who might take Charme to live there with him. Yet she didn't speak. Almost at once she knew that her revelation would not be welcomed. Memories were precious things. They shouldn't be brought up to date, their magic distilled with the mundane. He didn't like Charme. Her beauty meant nothing to him because he had seen greater beauty; had held in his arms women who had been far more enchanting.

He would, she was sure of it, have nothing in common with Eduard Talgarth. There was no hint of the sensitive in the Cornish skipper; he had said himself that he had no time for masquerade. He and Tarquin were as unalike as two men could be!

'Have you ever been back?' she asked curiously.

'No.' He smiled thoughtfully, and she felt a slight tightening of his arm around her. The swan glided by on its vigil and he watched it. 'There hasn't been the time, not since so much work caught up with me. There was drama school – I was lucky enough to win a place – and then Rep, where I carried scenery about until the director let me carry a spear. My first speaking part was in *Julius Caesar*. I played the soldier who has to stab Cassius, and now the role of Cassius is firmly established in my own repertoire. It's one of my favourites. I find the character deeper, more devious, than Antony or even Brutus. One can bring to the tent scene, on the battlefield, a lot of meaning and emotion.'

He gave a slight laugh and glanced down at Ruan. 'Am I boring you, Pierrette? You're very quiet.'

'I'm enthralled,' she said at once, and could not keep the betraying thrill out of her voice. 'Do go on!'

She heard him laugh again, softly. 'Are you starstruck, Ruan? Despite the freckles – and they're really rather charming – wouldn't you like to be an actress?'

'No.' She glanced up at him, still a little shy of him but unafraid that he would scoff at her ideas and find them unsophisticated. He could not be the actor he was if he didn't have much heart, and a sensitivity that he probably had to hide, even fight against, for the world of acting was a tough one, where hurt feelings had to be borne with a gay laugh, a nonchalant shrug of the shoulder.

'I like to watch,' she said, 'and I love to listen. I think really good actors are born, not made. They even have the right kind of faces – if you know what I mean?'

'Ravaged Greek gods, eh?'

'Yes.' They laughed together. 'Ann Destry is very lovely. The stage lights seem to catch in her hair. I loved that moment in *Othello* when you covered her throat with her long hair, as if to hide the marks of your fingers.'

'Ah, you noticed that?' He looked pleased. 'Yes, Ann is rather lovely and a good actress. I was lucky to get her for the season. The sandy young man you saw with her at the Mill Loft was Buckley Holt, her fiancé. He's making quite a name for himself as a stage designer. He isn't the regular sort of designer, but I won't go into that. Buck is all man, and he's produced some superb sets for our production of *Hamlet*, which we intend to put on towards the end of our stay at the Mask. It runs over four hours, and we decided on a spectacular staging. I'm not keen on modern variations of the play and great cubes that are meant to represent lord knows what! Our *Hamlet* will be as Elizabethan as if the author himself might stroll in to watch. It will be a highlight for me, Ruan – the first time I've played Hamlet.'

'I'm sure you will be great, Tarquin.'

'I want to be.' He spoke soberly. 'Just once in a lifetime an actor wants to give a performance that will be his memorial, if you understand me? He wants to know that long afterwards people will say, "Ah yes, I saw him play that part. He was unforgettable!" Actors are vain creatures, Pierrette. They want the adulation to continue even after the final curtain call.'

'Tarquin!' Something in his voice had struck a chill through her, and she saw that in the moonlight his face had a pensive look and his cheekbones seemed more hollowed. She wanted to put her arms around him, to make him safe, somehow. He was as vulnerable as her lonely self.

'Have I frightened you?' Abruptly his arms were holding her. 'Shall I take you home?'

'Yes, I must go home . . .' Her voice shook a little.

'And I should say good night and let it be good-bye.' He

paused, then added almost savagely, 'But I don't want that!
I want to see you again, Ruan, on Sunday. We'll drift in a
punt on the river and eat good things from a picnic hamper
– is it a date?'

'Yes . . . oh, yes!' Her eyes filled with a happy radiance.
'Where shall we meet, and shall I bring the food?'

'We'll meet at noon by the Mill Loft, where we can hire
a punt. I'll get a hamper from Lemon's. I seem to remember that they lay on quite a feast of turkey legs, *foie
gras* patties, and a bottle of wine.'

'You like everything done with style.' She smiled and
there was a wistfulness in her eyes, as if even yet she
couldn't believe that she fitted into his life, even for a few
short hours.

'I hope there isn't a boy-friend?' he murmured, half
teasingly. 'Some young Romeo—?'

'No.' She spoke quickly, too unworldly to hide her joy
in wanting to be with him. 'There is no one – and I'd like
very much to go on the river with you.'

'Good, it's settled. We'll drift with the tide, Ruan, and
let happen whatever is meant to happen.' And then before
she could speak he leaned forward and brushed his lips
against the little silver moon that clung to her thin young
cheek. 'You know, don't you, and you're just a child,' he
murmured.

'What do I know, Tarquin?' Her heart was beating
quickly, and she knew she could be hurt as never before if
she allowed herself to love this man. But she wanted to
love him. She would cherish each hour he gave her out of
his theatre life; live each day as it came, and if she died a
little when he went away, she would have lived as she had
never hoped to live.

'That my life has been lonely, Ruan, even in its most
crowded moments.' He smiled a little wryly. 'I'm not handing you a "line" and you know that as well. *Quelle pureté
d'âme.* You think with your heart, don't you?'

'Yes.' She thought of Catrina, who had done the same.
Only a few hours ago St. Cyr had said that she mustn't be

afraid of men because of her mother's mistake. How could she feel afraid in Tarquin's arms when she felt only happiness? She met his eyes fearlessly, and it was as they stood there, speaking with their eyes alone, that the moon was scarred by a cloud.

'I must take you home.' He said it with regret. 'It's going to rain again.'

It caught them as they ran laughing towards the house. Nearly all the cars were gone, several of the fairy lights had flickered out, and all that was left of the music was someone playing a record.

Tarquin's hand gripped Ruan's and then let it go. 'Don't forget,' he murmured.

'No.' Ruan swept off his cloak and handed it to him just as Ann Destry and her fiancé came out of the house.

'Quin – there you are! We'll give you a lift to the hotel.'

'I'm obliged, ma'am.' He swept her a bow, and at the same time Ruan felt the brush of his teasing eyes. Her heart skipped a beat. She hugged to herself the secret that was theirs. No one must know that Tarquin Powers meant to steal away with a girl on Sunday. The curiosity of other people could only spoil what to them was strangely enchanting. Amazement that he could find attractive a girl who was plain but for a pair of violet eyes would burst the bubble, dispel the magic, destroy a tenuous delight.

'Good night, everyone!' She ran indoors, and felt the look that followed her from Ann Destry. She met Charme in the hall, saying good night to someone so tall and dark he was unmistakable.

'Ruan?'

'Lovely party, Charme!' Her smile was gay, mischievous; a warmth for everyone flowed from her heart. 'Did you enjoy yourself, Mr. Talgarth?'

She half turned on the stairs to look at him. Her hair was rain-straight, her eyes were shining, and still the little moon clung silver to her cheek.

'Did you, Miss Perry?' he countered, and she knew from his eyes – so penetrating – that he had seen her depart with

Tarquin.

'Yes, it was fun.' A little flash of defiance lit her eyes, for what right had he, this stranger, to look disapproving? As the little stepsister was she supposed to sit in a corner and have nothing, nobody, no delight but charity from the St. Cyrs? All at once she was shaken by anger. She could have struck at this man's face, with its bones like rocks under the sea-browned skin. She hated him! He was arrogant . . . one of those who thought that only the beautiful were meant for love.

'Will you be staying long in Avendon?' she asked coldly. 'Or can't you wait to get back to your chateau?'

His eyes narrowed, and for this brief electrical moment they were alone while Charme was held in conversation by friends of her father's. He stood below Ruan, looking up the white-painted stairs at her slender figure, his brows a black dangerous line, his eyes burning blue in all that darkness.

'There are two kinds of people,' he said softly. 'They are the tame and the wild, and if you ever come to Cornwall, I shall teach you what manner of man I am.'

'I have you summed up already,' she said recklessly. 'And I have no intention of ever coming to visit you and your wife.'

'I have no wife, Miss Perry.'

'But you will have, won't you, Mr. Talgarth?' She swung on her heel and raced up the stairs, aware that he went on standing where she left him, dark, so very dark against the pale woodwork, the blue carpet like a sea pool under his feet, a gleam of onyx at his cuff as he slicked from his eyes that black streak of hair.

She knew what manner of man he was, and she almost pitied Charme who would have to cope with him. He might be generous with his gifts, but he was not the sort to uproot himself for the sake of a woman, even one he might desire. The woman would have to go his way, and Ruan couldn't picture her stepsister in the wilds of Cornwall, even as mistress of a chateau built long ago by a princely

43

rebel.

A storm was in the air, Ruan thought, as she stood at her window and ran her hands through her rain-tousled hair.

'Tarquin.' She murmured his name, and curled down into the window seat. A breeze stole in and kissed her cheek, and remembering his kiss she forgot Eduard Talgarth and the anger he had aroused in her.

In four days' time she would see Tarquin again.

CHAPTER THREE

Now each Sunday they were meeting to spend the day together, and there was so much to be discovered, so many things of beauty that took on an added charm because they shared them together. He enjoyed handling the punt they hired, and the Avon wended its way through some of the loveliest country, where they ate their lunch on a riverbank, or strolled as far as one of the Tudor inns with an old-world frontage of plaster and timbering and mullioned windows, where they sat in one of the parlours and ate roast beef and browned potatoes while the sun streamed in past the climbing geraniums.

She was learning how much the theatre took out of him, how much he needed to relax with someone like her, who made no demands on him, who listened and laughed and explored with him the old water-mills, the ruins of castles, the golden heart of England. They wandered in cherry orchards, took footpaths that rambled over the hills and led to the remains of an old Roman vineyard, or to a creamy-walled cottage topped by a crusty brown thatch. An enchanted cottage with low cobbled garden walls overhung by clumps of greenery spattered with butter-yellow flowers. There was lavender and ice-plant glittering against a burnt-gold plant. A perfect little house. A picture and a dream with its windows fresh with net and little copper jugs.

They didn't speak as they made their way back to the river and the punt, where she looked at him with a smile of grave charm, her hair blowing above her eyes, boyish in her canvas jeans and leaf-green shirt.

He took her hand and kissed it lightly. 'Dear nymph, you read my heart, don't you? You know it's torn two ways.'

She nodded and her smile didn't falter. Though his kiss

had not yet touched her lips, she sensed that he was never completely happy; that something stood between them.

He handed her into the punt, lean and agile in fawn trousers and a white shirt, and as she took her seat she watched the way he handled the punt pole, his movements as supple as they were on stage. Everything about him seemed designed to make of a stage role a thing of magic, and when he acted he was someone apart from her – he was Cassius, watching the storm and speaking of 'the strange impatience of the heavens'.

Their punt floated on the sunlit river and everything but the water was still and softly hazy. Their eyes met, and in a moment there was a certain beauty in her smile.

'You're a rare creature, Ruan,' he said. 'Did I ever tell you that nature was kind enough to give you flowers for eyes?'

He often said such things with easy grace, and she didn't dare to let them be a substitute for words of affection. It would be self-delusion to let herself believe that he had fallen in love with a country girl who knew so little of his world. His need was for a companion; someone with whom he could be carefree.

That evening when they parted on the old weir bridge (she kept secret from the St. Cyrs her meetings with Tarquin) he suddenly produced a ring in the shape of a blue scarab, with an inscription under the wing.

'For friendship,' he said, but he slipped it on the finger men choose for their ring of love, and it was unbearable, as if he played a game with her. 'No – I don't want it!' She wrenched the ring from her finger and threw it at his feet, then she turned and ran from him and she meant never to see him again ... to be friends was not enough ... it was not fun any more.

'Ruan?'

She ran on across the bridge and the dying blaze of the sun was in her eyes, and the tears, and before she could save herself she stumbled down the two wide steps at the foot of the bridge and fell headlong into the tall grass and the clumps of wild flowers.

'Ruan!' He was beside her, kneeling in the grass, catching hold of her. His face was grim and concerned, and beside his mouth a nerve beat quickly, visible to her eyes as he pulled her against him, pulled her close to the warmth of his skin where his shirt was open at his throat.

'No – please!' She struggled with him. He wanted only a pal – his dear nymph. 'I'm all right ... let me up and let me go home.'

But he went on holding her, and the tang of grass and thyme and crushed petals was an incense all around them. 'No ...' It was a husky whisper, and the next instant she felt the warm crush of his arms and saw his face draw near in the dusk, and it was as if each feature had been etched by the point of a star. The breath caught in her throat and the first light touch of his lips on hers was not to be believed in ... until suddenly the warmth was flame and the caress was gone, to be replaced by the hunger of a man who had waited with pent-up longing for this moment.

The weir rushed on, and her lips, her eyes, the pulse in her throat, all were at the mercy of his kisses. The floodgates had opened and the tide swept over her, until at last she begged, half laughing, and just a little frightened, that he please stop or she would die of the kissing.

He held her strongly and closely to his warmth, and as the sky darkened the stars came out one by one. Ruan watched them and felt a happiness that seemed poised on a waiting edge.

'You're such a sweet thing,' he murmured. 'I knew it from the moment I saw you standing below the stage in that half-dark theatre, holding that absurd little dog in your arms. I saw innocence and trust and I swore to myself that I wouldn't touch you. I meant us to have only these friendly afternoons together. I meant not to break the gentle spell of these hours on the river.'

She couldn't speak, couldn't ask why the kissing was dangerous. She lay looking at him, cradled by his firm arm, and in the radiance from the river she saw how drawn and tense his face was.

'Pierrette,' he spoke the name in her tumbled hair, 'don't you know, haven't you guessed why I've fought this ... told myself we could be friends but nothing more? It was a bungling thing, to go and put the ring on the one finger that can never wear a ring of mine.'

She listened to the tumbling of the weir, and to the beating of her heart, and all at once the truth began to take torturing shape, spelling out the words before he spoke them.

'I'm married, Ruan.' He said it harshly. 'Didn't you ever wonder? Didn't you ever ask yourself why I never kissed you? Did you think I didn't find you attractive enough?'

Married?

The pealing of evening bells from a nearby church took on the sound of a knell, and the scents of the dying day turned bittersweet on the air as the shock of his revelation spread through her.

'No one – ever mentions your wife, Tarquin.'

'Only my closest friends know I have one.' With a sigh he helped Ruan to her feet and by unspoken consent they returned to the bridge. He took a lighter from his pocket and played the small light over the spot where they had been standing, and after a moment's search he found the ring which she had flung at his feet ... as if warned by some instinct that it was wrong of him to give her a ring.

'Please, Ruan.' He held it out to her. 'On any finger you like. What does it matter? We have to be friends again, even though we care for each other in a deeper sense.'

'Why does no one speak of your wife?' She had to ask; she had to know all the secret. 'Are you separated from her?'

He unclosed her slender fingers and pressed the ring into her hand. 'We don't live together – any more. We married when I was just an aspiring actor, and four years later she became ill and had to be sent away to a home for nervous diseases, a place that looks like a Californian ranch.'

He sighed deeply. 'She's Italian, quite beautiful, and hopelessly beyond the reach of ever becoming my wife again – and yet until one of us dies she is for all time my wife. I was so crazy about her at the time we married that I took her faith. You understand what that means, Ruan?'

'Yes.' It was but a whisper, and her hands were shaking as she slipped the blue scarab ring on to her right middle finger. She would wear it always. It was all she might have of him. 'Yes, I understand all the implications, Tarquin, and I'm so sorry for you. I thought I didn't fit into your world of the theatre – and then again I thought myself too young, too naïve, even too plain—'

'Darling nymph,' he took her by the shoulders and his grip was painful in its intensity, 'how could you be plain with violet eyes? How could you not bewitch me with your smile that holds none of the artifice I see every day of my life – except on these days with you? These precious hoarded Sundays. These river trips I shall not forget.'

'You talk as if you're going away, Tarquin.' It took all her courage, all her control, not to cry.

'I belong to the greasepaint and the mask, my dear. I give myself to the crowd like a gladiator to the lions ... and now you know why. Never the twain shall meet, yet we met, and I should have sent you away and tried no more to see you. That foolish party! I couldn't resist the invitation when someone said that Charme St. Cyr had a sister named Ruan. Could there be two girls in Avendon with a name so rare? I had to find out! Then I saw you, in that pierrot outfit, *my* Ruan, clean and fresh as rain on the young green leaves of springtime. I blighted my own springtime and should have stayed away from you ...'

'I don't regret anything. Not a moment, not an hour.' She smiled into his eyes, for nothing he had said had really blighted the magic of knowing him; it wouldn't just die because there was no future for them together. Why, she asked herself, must they part and walk away from each other, lonely again?

'There are two more weeks before you play Hamlet,' she

49

said softly. 'Two more Sundays for us to be together. Don't let's throw them away.'

'It could now be dangerous,' he warned her. 'I'm only a man and when we're alone – Pierrette, you aren't a child!'

'No.' She shook her head. 'I'm suddenly so much older and wiser, and I couldn't bear to be robbed of one single moment of the time we have left to share. You said we'd go to Stratford next week, remember?'

'I think I was on the way to going to the devil before you came along.' He closed his arms around her and pressed his cheek to her windblown hair. 'I fly to Rome after *Hamlet*, to make a film. These things I have to do because I need the money for Nina. It will be that way for years, with people wondering why I give a quarter of my time to the theatre when I long to give all of it.'

'My poor Tarquin.' She drew his head down to her and there on the weir bridge they kissed with a passionate sadness, the gems of the scarab ring playing a blue light over his lean cheek.

She arrived home in a pensive mood, to find the house full of Charme's friends. The record-player was belting out the latest dance number, and a couple were swinging their hips to it in the brightly lit hall.

'Isn't it splendid news?' Someone she vaguely knew was smiling all over his face and holding a glass of champagne in his hand . . . she could see the bubbles rising to the brim. 'Charme is going to be married! She and the lucky chap made up their minds today.'

Married – Charme?

Ruan glanced round dazedly, her mind and her heart still at the mercy of what Tarquin had revealed . . . that he had a wife in America, young, lovely, but an invalid.

'I – I've been out all day. I didn't know about the engagement.' Ruan stood hesitant on the stairs, and heard from the direction of the lounge the merry sounds of laughter and clinking wine glasses. She should go in and add her congratulations, but somehow she couldn't make the effort. She had felt certain that Eduard Talgarth had left Avendon several days ago, but he must have returned for the occasion.

'Simon's always had a silver spoon in his mouth.' There was a laugh, followed by the raising of the champagne glass. 'Here's to them! May they always be the town's leading lights.'

Simon? Simon and Charme!

Ruan leaned weakly against the stair rail and she could have laughed aloud for ever supposing that her stepsister would give up the heir to a flourishing furniture business to go and live in the wilds of Cornwall. It was now so obvious that Charme and Talgarth had never been suited, her stepsister so in love with the good life and the Cornishman so rugged, with a sea light in his eyes and an air about him of being the captain of his own fate.

Her stepsister and Simon Fox had in common their love of gaiety and good times, and in the younger man Charme would have a husband she could lead about by the nose. Ruan couldn't imagine the dark, arrogant Talgarth being led about by anyone. The last time she had seen him had been in the shop where she worked. He had strolled in to buy a porcelain figure of a girl holding to her head a wind-blown hat with a wide brim, wearing a crinoline and slippers of scarlet. It had been expensive, and Ruan had felt like saying that Charme would prefer a piece of jewellery or an attractive powder-box.

He had stood at the other side of the counter, over-powering among the ornaments, some of which were as delicate as shell. 'I see you are advertising the Mask plays in the window,' he had drawled. 'You seem to be a regular playgoer. Whenever I call at the villa you are never at home.'

'I've always been fond of the theatre,' she had said, on the defensive as always with the man. 'It's especially exciting when famous actors come for the season.'

'Be careful, Ruan. One of them might throw stardust in your eyes and it could be painful.' With this remark he had left and she had not seen him again. But in the next fortnight she sometimes thought of his words when allowed backstage at the Mask. She became quite friendly with Ann Destry, who didn't mince her words either.

'We meet all sorts,' she said, as she and Ruan stood in the wings together. 'It's a well-known fact that girls in the various towns develop crushes on actors, and we get a laugh out of it, but you're different, Ruan.'

'Well, thanks.' Ruan gazed at the rehearsal on stage. 'I'm not running after Tarquin.'

'Buck and I know that. We know how he feels about you – to the rest of the cast he's the aloof and magnificent Quin Powers, but to us he's a friend. Ruan, you're not the kind of girl to want an affair with a man, and Quin can't legalize what you and he feel for each other. Could you face being his mistress?'

It was a question Ruan winced at. In the privacy of her thoughts she shrank from the answer, but when she was with Tarquin nothing seemed to matter except that she make him happy, be whatever he wished her to be ... his mistress in Rome if he wanted that. He would never ask it of her here in Avendon, where she lived and worked, but as the days drew nearer for his departure from Avendon, she had the feeling that he might ask her to go abroad with him.

It was in his eyes, the clasp of his arms, unspoken in his kiss. He wanted an end to loneliness ... he wanted her.

Their mood was one of a shared tenseness on the day they visited Stratford, stopping off to take lunch at a castle-like inn smothered in ivy. There was an ancient Roman well in the garden where they ate their meal, and he suggested that he take a photograph of her posed against the lichened stone.

'Is it for your album of memories?' she asked, meaning to be gay and bright, but striking the wrong note. His eyes flashed to meet hers, the pupils expanding as he came deliberately to her, took her by the chin and bruised the smile from her lips.

'If I were a Roman of old and you my slave girl, then there would be no talk of memories, or of partings.' He spoke close to her, as savagely as he had kissed her, and she caught at the rim of the Roman well, slim and girlish in a dress patterned with willow green leaves and bronze petals. She gasped, half-frightened, as Tarquin suddenly kissed the curve of her neck.

'Tarquin, let's make a move,' she spoke breathlessly. 'Some other people have come into the garden . . . please!'

'Please?' he mocked. 'The rules have to be obeyed, don't they?'

'W-what rules?'

'Those of convention, my sweet. Or are you afraid of my love all of a sudden?'

'You're being cruel!'

'Love is cruel.' He took hold of her and pulled her out of sight of the three people who were taking a table for lunch in this old-world garden. He found for them seclusion near some espalier pear trees, old and twisted. Below the wall, against the ground, ran a drift of wild violets, and for a long moment Tarquin stared at them, and then slowly he looked up and his gaze sank deep into Ruan's eyes that were the colour of the flowers.

'Why pretend that it's easy being friends?' he murmured. 'We look at each other, Ruan, and other people just don't exist. Will you deny it, little witch *d'amour*, when your violet eyes drown me in them each time I look at you?'

'No . . .' She could make no denials when her eyes spoke for her. 'But what I feel frightens me a little, Tarquin.'

'Ah, Ruan.' His hand became caressive on her russet hair. 'Do you think I don't get frightened, dear nymph? Do you think I want to know the pain of saying good-bye to you, someone I have found who seems to belong to no one but me? Someone I must leave who will find love, perhaps, with another man?' He laid his cheek against her hair, and the scent of the wild flowers seemed to add to the poignancy, so that Ruan would never see or breathe them without remembering this moment.

As Tarquin's arms tightened around her, she knew instinctively what he meant to ask of her. There was something fateful about their being here. The old trees, a passing cloud, a little breath of coldness through the garden, all were part of the moment as if the stage were set for his question, and her answer.

'I want you to come to Rome with me,' he said. 'I can't face any more loneliness. The emptiness of not having someone I need, who needs and cares for me as a person rather than a public image. I want you to come with me very much, Ruan.'

It was his use of the word loneliness that touched her heart and melted it. It was another term for being without love, without someone to whom you truly mattered . . . her joy in being needed by him would be her armour against the sin of it.

His hand rested near her cheek and she turned her head and shyly pressed her lips to the lean fingers, feeling the pressure of his signet ring with its bloodstone. The silent kiss was her answer without word, catching his sense of symbolism. With a gesture he could express a sadness, a delight, or a surrender.

'My dear!' He swept her close to him, held her against the espalier trees, and the thrill of his kiss ran all through her. His tender words broke in little waves against her throat, and she let herself hear nothing but those words. She strove not to see any face but his . . . Catrina's with its reproach would be too much to bear . . . and there was another, dark, strong and Celtic, warning her, which she pushed away from her, as if physically. It was her life. There was no one else but Tarquin who really cared about her. It wouldn't matter to the St. Cyrs if she slipped out of their circle, into which she had never fitted.

'Tarquin, we'd better be making a move.'

'Yes — I suppose we must.' But the threat of another kiss shimmered in his eyes, and with a breathless laugh she pulled free of him and ran pursued through the garden.

54

People gazed after them from the lunch tables.

'Did you see!' someone exclaimed. 'That was the actor we saw the other evening in *School For Scandal*!'

'The girl as well?'

'Very likely. They're so made up on stage.'

Ruan gave a wry smile as Tarquin opened the door of the small car he had hired for their drive to Stratford. '*Scandal*,' he said dramatically.

Ruan hung on to her smile as he started the car and they swung out of the lane on to the highway. He was a fast driver and an hour later they were swooping over Clopton Bridge, picturesque with its mellow row of arches. The gleaming river and green trees on its banks followed the road to the Memorial Theatre and soon it towered in sight, like a great liner afloat on the water.

They parked the car and strolled across the lawns towards the cubistic building, so outwardly modern, and yet the home of great language and plays written centuries ago.

'The last time I was here,' mused Tarquin, 'I played Mercutio in *Romeo and Juliet*.'

'I wish I could have seen you.' Ruan smiled at him, the sun reflecting from the water on to her bright unruly hair. Forgotten for a while were her misgivings. It gave only pleasure that other people gazed after his tall, supple figure, noticing him for somebody out of the ordinary with his fine face.

Whatever his private torments, he was before anything else an English actor of the first rank, with a dash of the foreign in him from the past, and from his mother who had come from the mystic isles of Arran.

'Tell me more about it,' she coaxed. 'Was it exciting to act on one of the great stages here at the Memorial?'

'Wonderful. I enjoyed playing Mercutio, but would have made an unlikely Romeo.' He chuckled. 'Romeo is the eternal boy lover, and actors should cease to play him after the age of twenty-four. Were you aware, Ruan, that I'm thirty-four?'

'I suspected it,' she said lightly.

'Don't you mind?' He gripped her hand in his. 'You're so young, but a mere Juliet. Have you no wish to be wooed by a Romeo?'

'I much prefer Petruchio.'

'You're no Kate for temper.' His grey eyes smiled as they took her in. 'There is a physical resemblance, however. *"Kate like the hazel twig is straight and slender and as brown in hue as hazel nuts and sweeter than the kernels."* '

'Do you always say such nice things to your Kates?' she asked, with a flash of curiosity.

'There have not been so many, Ruan.'

'I know.' Her fingers curled in among his, for always the shadow of Nina would haunt his happiness, and hers.

The library and picture gallery of the Memorial had escaped the fire that had gutted the old theatre. It remained attached in the old style to the modern, and there they looked at costumes and manuscripts, and paintings of famous performers. A brooding Hamlet holding the skull. Antony in wonderful Roman robes, with an amulet against his chest. There was Olivier as Othello, a passionate and startling portrait.

'The finest performance of this day and age,' said Tarquin with feeling. 'It will go down in theatre history as a portrayal more alive, more intense than anything achieved since Edmund Keane died. Olivier has his memorial. He's a great, great actor.'

A thrill ran through Ruan as Tarquin spoke. He knew so much about his profession, cared so deeply that he give always of his best, longed in his turn to be a great and stirring performer. She was sure that he would be; that one day people would walk through this gallery and worship his portrait.

She looked at him as he regarded the brooding Hamlet in sombre costume, outlined against the battlements of a castle. The play would be Tarquin's farewell performance at the Mask, and then with him she would say good-bye to Avendon. She told herself ardently that they'd be happy –

as happy as possible!

'Come,' he gathered her arm through his, 'let us go and look at Anne Hathaway's cottage, like a proper pair of tourists, and then we'll spend the evening at the Mill Loft with Buckley and his Ann.'

They walked together down the gallery, past Romeo in his deeply open silk shirt, past Macbeth in his strange crown and chain, past the severe and beautiful face of Coriolanus. At the doorway they turned for a last look and the afternoon sunlight fell on the armour and the cloaks. 'It's a world apart,' Ruan murmured.

'It will be your world when you come to me,' said Tarquin, his voice extra deep, his brilliant eyes holding hers in captivity. She nodded, just a little terrified by what he implied. In Rome she would belong completely to Tarquin ... there the die would be cast.

They walked in silence to the car, and drove without haste to see the cottage in which Shakespeare's wife had lived. It had an old-world garden full of hollyhocks and sunflowers. The long timber and plaster front of the house was bent over with age, and the windows were latticed beneath the thatched roof. So still and old, so that even the visitors who wandered in and out of the low-beamed rooms could not spoil completely the peace of a place lived in long ago by those who had known the greatest of all writers.

As the sun dipped lower in the sky Ruan breathed the scent of the flowers, always stronger as day waned, and then she became aware that a group of people had recognized Tarquin and were asking for his autograph. She watched as he exchanged a few easy words with them and signed his name with a flourish on their Stratford catalogues and car maps.

One young woman was looking at him with eyes that shone with admiration, and Ruan remembered her own first meeting with Tarquin. Had she looked like that, so ready to adore him? Was that why he had been tempted to come to Charme's party? Was that the reason he wanted her, because she was so innocently adoring, and the sort not to intrude into his public life?

Oh, she was being sensitive! She couldn't expect Tarquin to pull her forward and say outright, 'This is the girl I have chosen to share my life.' He could never say it in plain terms. He was not free to do so, and then with his inimitable smile he bade his admirers good-bye and strode to Ruan. She was aware of the women's eyes assessing her dress and her figure, wondering if she could be an actress, one they ought to recognize.

'Sweetheart?'

She smiled up at him. 'What does it feel like to be admired by women wherever you go?'

'As if they'd like to slice me up, share me out and keep me as a souvenir in serviettes.'

She laughed, and felt his arm twine lightly around her waist as they made for the car. Those people watched and wondered, and she knew with a warm thrill that Tarquin was letting them know that she was someone special . . . his possession.

His lips brushed her hair as he put her into the car. 'It's like you, Ruan, brave and bright as a sunflower,' he said softly.

She met his eyes and realized that the empathy between them made their thoughts readable to each other. He knew that for a few minutes she had felt forlornly separated from him by the barrier of his fame, and he reassured her with a kiss, a look deep into her eyes. So would it be, time and time again, he silently warned her. She must accept it, if she chose to accept him.

They drove off as the sun was dipping low, a ball of flame in the sky, setting fire with beauty the rolling fields and blossoming hedgerows. Birds called in the branches of the trees, and Ruan was sure she heard a cuckoo calling as they sped along a lane dappled by the red sun and the purpling shadows of evening.

'Make a wish!' she said quickly. 'I hear the cuckoo.'

'You child!' he grinned. 'There, I've made one. Shall I

tell you—?'

'No, it won't come true if you reveal it.'

'It's half true already, dear nymph.'

She knew at once what he meant, and with a quickly beating, happy-apprehensive heart she snuggled down beside him and rested her cheek against the bristly tweed of his jacket.

Darkness fell before they reached the Mill Loft, where they had arranged to meet Ann and Buckley for supper. Ruan stirred out of the half-dream into which she had fallen, and said drowsily: 'Oh, look at the stars. They're so still, so far away, they frighten me a little.'

'You strange girl,' said Tarquin.

'I bet you wouldn't say that to all your adoring fans.'

'My adoring fans, as you call them, wouldn't be half-asleep in my pocket, tempting a stalled car with unflattering observations about the stars.'

'Are they up there for a special purpose, then?'

'Would you like me to demonstrate?'

'And keep Ann and Buckley waiting?'

'We can always say the car felt like a rest.' With a smooth braking movement Tarquin stopped the car by the roadside. He turned swiftly to Ruan and gathered to him her slim figure warmed by his own closeness. He kissed her teasingly, as he had spoken, then suddenly his arms tightened to the point of pain, and a little to her alarm a tremor shook him.

'Ruan – Ruan darling, is it fair of me to ask you to give up everything for my sake? Your home, your chance of meeting someone who can give you his name—?'

'I love you,' she touched his lean cheek. 'I'm not afraid of the future, and the St. Cyr house has never been my home in the sense that you mean. I have never truly belonged, as I want to belong to you.'

'And I, little one, would like to bind you to me with a ring of gold.' He kissed her eyes, the small hollow in her cheek, the lobe of her ear. 'I'm sure of how I feel, Ruan, because I'm older than you, and because of my marriage.

But are you so sure about your own feelings? It isn't just stardust—?'

Her heart thumped ... be careful ... stardust in your eyes could be painful. ...

'No!' The word broke from her lips. She buried her face in Tarquin's shoulder, held tightly to his warmth and his lean strength. 'I'm sure of nothing except in your arms. You make me welcome, you make me feel needed. There's no one else to whom I mean anything. No one else who wants me—'

'Then are you mistaking loneliness for love, Ruan?'

'Kiss me,' she whispered, 'and find your own answer.'

It was late when Ruan let herself into the St. Cyr house. A lamp glimmered low in the lounge, and as she would have passed by the door on her way to the stairs, a voice called out: 'Is that you, Ruan?' A pause followed, as if Charme glanced at the clock. 'Come in a moment. I want to talk to you.'

Ruan had been expecting the summons for several days, ever since she and Tarquin had been seen by friends of Charme eating pastries at Lemon's. Tarquin had been popping a candied cherry into her mouth at the time, and with a resigned smile she pushed open the door of the lounge and went in to face the inquisition.

Charme sat on one of the twin sofas, smoking a cigarette in a short ivory holder. Even alone she was poised and elegant, a blue cushion behind her head to set off her coronet of pale-gold hair. She wore a short evening dress of blue embroidered with softly sparkling beads.

Ruan had always thought her stepsister beautiful ... and had wished so often that her nature matched her looks. If they had, then life at the villa would have been a little happier. But there was a streak of the leopardess in Charme. She didn't like members of her own sex who were uninterested in clothes, looks, and the scandals of a small town. She found in Ruan a woodsy creature on whom it was a secret pleasure to try her claws ... long and polished by the light of the blue-shaded sofa lamp.

'Where have you been?' she asked pleasantly. 'It's very late, and not the first time you've crept in hoping we wouldn't hear you.'

'I don't creep in,' Ruan denied. 'I'd come in through the back way if I wanted to avoid you or your father.'

'You're quite brazen about it, then?'

'What do you mean?' Ruan stood taut in front of her stepsister, her hair a russet glimmer about her face, from which all the colour had suddenly fled.

'You know full well what I mean.' Charme lifted her cigarette and drew deliberately on the ivory mouthpiece. 'I imagine by now that half of Avendon is aware of your relationship with that actor from the Mask Theatre.'

Ruan caught her breath . . . Charme made it sound as if she were having an affair with Tarquin . . . moved to spite because his interest was centred on someone less decorative than herself. He had come to her party, but only to see Ruan. He had made available to the younger girl the fascinating company at the Mask. He had taken her to lunch at Lemon's, and to supper at the Mill. He had preferred her friendship to that of the more élite of Avendon.

The wide violet eyes of Ruan met the hazel-gold of Charme's, saw they were narrowed like a cat's. She meant to scratch deep, and to make the younger girl suffer for being more attractive to the worldly actor than her elegant self. She wore Simon Fox's diamond ring, and had captured the attention of the dark personage from Cornwall, but still she wanted more.

'Don't you think you're making a little fool of yourself, hanging after a man so much older than yourself?' The words came cuttingly from the red lips that could look thin in anger. 'Everyone knows that actors can turn the heads of plain, silly girls, flattered by a few attentions, and it wouldn't please Father and myself if you brought home any trouble. There's bound to be promiscuity in your blood, but we've tried to keep you from going the way of your mother—'

'I wouldn't say any more, Charme!' Ruan's eyes were brilliant with her own anger. 'I'll black your eye if you say one more nasty thing about Catrina. Say what you like about me! I'm used to it, and I know better than anyone that I haven't done anything wrong in seeing Tarquin and spending with him the most pleasant and interesting hours of my life. He's cultured and kind, and one of our finest actors ... not a slick seducer from some third-rate touring company!'

'You're smitten with the man,' Charme drawled. 'I suppose with someone as naïve as a kid of nineteen, with no appeal for younger men, he can play the great actor to perfection. I thought the cream of the profession went to Stratford to act. Isn't he good enough for the Memorial?'

'He appeared at Stratford long before he became famous enough to pick and choose his theatre. The Mask appeals to him for its beauty and the effective way a classical play can be performed on its more intimate stage—' Ruan broke off at the slow, sarcastic raising of her stepsister's eyebrows. Charme had no interest in the theatre, and to her the word intimate meant only one thing.

'What are you going to do when your hero leaves Avendon?' she inquired mockingly. 'He won't marry you. He knows you couldn't fit into his sophisticated world. You'd be a liability. He only wants you while he's here in Avendon because you flatter his ego. What actor could resist being thought wonderful, on and off the stage?'

Oh, what pleasure it would have given Ruan to retort that she was going with Tarquin when he left Avendon, but she kept her lips firmly locked. When the time came she would leave quietly, with few regrets. Charme had shown her tonight that she was more unwanted than ever before. She had become a rival. Though not pretty in the accepted sense, a slim, woodsy thing with eyes that sometimes looked too big for her face, she had attracted a powerfully attractive man ... and Charme was jealous.

With her new awareness of life and love, Ruan sensed

62

that her stepsister was not in love with Simon Fox. She was driven to marry a man she could rule, otherwise she would have chosen the dark and dominant stranger from Cornwall. It infuriated her that Ruan was free of ambition; unafraid to let her heart be her guide.

Ruan tensed as Charme came to her feet, a head taller, outwardly lovely in her blue dress, the ring on her left hand flashing with solitaire fire.

'If you get yourself into trouble,' she said spitefully, 'don't come running to me or Father. Little fool, no man of the world would want you for anything else but his amusement. Look at you! Unstyled hair all over the place. No figure to speak of. Lips a schoolgirl pink ... or has it all been kissed off in the back of a car in some country lane?'

This stab in the dark was painfully near the truth, and yet so far removed from the tender torment of those moments in Tarquin's arms, when he had asked her to be sure that she loved him. When he had spoken of stardust in her eyes, blinding her to what she truly wanted. She looked at Charme, and her eyes were wide open to the future, to its possible heartaches, and its promise of happiness. Here at the villa she was treated like a charity child who was in the way.

'You don't have to worry, Charme,' she said quietly. 'If I ever need help or sympathy, I shan't come to you. I'd sooner go to a stranger.'

She turned on her heel and as she walked from the lounge the clock on the mantelpiece began to chime. When she reached her room it was midnight. The hour of the witch, and of Cinderella's return to earth with her dress in tatters. Ruan closed the door behind her and switched on the light. Her reflection sprang at her from the dressing-table mirror. Her face was pale, and her hair was tousled by Tarquin's touch.

He had said of her hair that it was brave and bright as a sunflower.

He had surely meant it ... it couldn't be true that she

merely flattered him with her youthful worship.

'I want you,' he had said. 'I can't face any more the loneliness of not having someone who needs me . . . for myself.'

Was being wanted the same as being loved?

CHAPTER FOUR

FRIDAY was one of those sultry days with a promise of thunder in the air. Ruan came to work in a sleeveless dress of a pale mauve colour, and her hair was looped back in a mauve ribbon. Her eyes held captive a brave, bright smile.

'Looks like we're in for a storm,' remarked the young woman who worked with her in the shop. 'That's the trouble with this country of ours. As soon as we have a run of fine weather we pay for it with lashings of rain. It's bound to come. I can feel a little nerve hammering in my temple – do you get that feeling when there's thunder about, Ruan?'

'Mmm.' Ruan was unpacking some antique items their boss had bought at an auction. 'I hope it rains before to-night. I have a date to go to the theatre.'

The other girl gave her a knowing look. 'It's *Hamlet* tonight, isn't it?'

'Yes.' Ruan smiled and felt her quickening heart. She dusted a bronze figure of a knight on horseback. 'Leonard is charging well for this item. Do you like it, Kay?'

'It's all right, but I prefer something a bit more up to date. Where did he get that lot?'

'At the sell-up of that big manor house at Henley-in-Arden.'

'It's a shame the way those lovely old places are going up for sale. I suppose their owners can't afford their upkeep. I mean, all those rooms, and girls won't work as housemaids unless they get good wages. Mr. St. Cyr must be quite well-off, Ruan. I mean, you have those two foreign girls and a woman for the cooking. And your sister doesn't go to work.'

'She isn't my sister,' Ruan said, her hands clenching about a green glass goblet.

'No, I forgot. You aren't alike enough to be real sisters. Has she said yet when the wedding is to take place – lucky girl, to have nabbed someone whose father owns a furniture business!'

'I expect I shall read the announcement in the local paper with everyone else.' Ruan's smile came back. 'We're not exactly on confiding terms.'

'She always strikes me as being a bit haughty,' Kay admitted. 'But I do envy her gorgeous blonde hair. It's natural, of course?'

'Every shining hair – ah, here comes a customer! You serve him, Kay.' Ruan's dimple was spiced. 'I know you're keen on the Texan type!'

The morning passed without event, and still the sun was gilt and sultrily warm. Came lunchtime and Kay went off to her pie and chips while Ruan stayed behind to read a magazine and eat sandwiches. A tourist lunching at Lemon's might notice something in the window of the Antique Shoppe, so they didn't close but took turns working through the lunch hour. Neither of the girls really minded. The shop was a pleasant place, and Lemon's next door always a source of interest with its cavalcade of visitors, bluff Americans with their smart wives, and worldly Europeans. Londoners with their lively eyes, and bronzed Australians who looked slightly awkward, as if about to crack their tall heads on the quaint beams of the famous restaurant.

Ruan was reading idly a story about love on a tropical island, when the bell of the shop tinkled and she glanced up expecting to see a customer. Instead she was confronted by a messenger boy toting an enormous basket of violets, a mass of purple and white scenting out the shop as the boy grinned at her.

'Miss Perry?' he wanted to know.

'Y-yes.'

'Then you're the lady.' He placed the basket of flowers on the counter and put beside them a smartly wrapped box finished off with a silk bow. 'Happy returns, miss.'

'It isn't my birthday,' she said in bewilderment.

But the boy was gone and she was alone with her tributes. She searched the basket for a card, but couldn't find one.

She opened the ribboned box and found inside a beautiful bottle filled with *Violette des sorciers*, a French perfume both expensive and exciting. With the perfume there was a small envelope and inside a little card with a flourish of words in an unmistakable hand.

'To the girl whose eyes are more lovely than a garden of violets. I will see you tonight, dear nymph, until then *au 'voir*, Tarquin.'

Tears sprang into her eyes. How like him! How gallant and kind to remember her today of all days, when the final rehearsal for *Hamlet* was under way, the most important role of the season for Tarquin, and his farewell salute to Avendon. For three nights he would play the part, and then on Tuesday morning they would drive to the airport, for all the arrangements were now made for their departure. All that remained was for Ruan to tell her stepfather that she was going away.

She dabbed on a little of the cool perfume, and fondled the violets, their petals like velvet, reminding her of the garden at Stratford, where Tarquin had said passionately that love could be cruel.

He had been thinking of Nina, the woman who would like a shadow share their days and their nights. It could not be otherwise, and only Ruan's tender love for Tarquin made it possible for her to go with him to Rome, there to make a little happiness for him.

'What's all this?' Kay had come in suddenly, and she stood gaping at the great spill of violets over the counter of the shop. They lit it up and reflected in the copper surfaces of jugs and bowls. They merged their colour with Ruan's eyes as she gazed over the counter at Kay.

'A friend sent them.' A smile came and went on her lips, for the other girl looked so amazed. 'Lovely, aren't they?'

'Perfume as well?' Kay sniffed appreciatively. 'Mmmm, from Hamlet?'

'Yes.'

'You love him till it hurts, don't you, Ru?' Kay touched the violets. 'Are you wise to keep on seeing him? It'll hurt more when he leaves, you know.'

Ruan had not told anyone, yet, that she was going away with Tarquin. She had given in her notice, but had not given any reason for quitting her job. Leonard Wells had shrugged his shoulders. Shop assistants were easily replaceable in Avendon, but Ruan knew that Kay would be upset to hear she was leaving.

She might at this moment have spoken, but there was a sudden influx of souvenir-hunters, and it wasn't until after four that they found time to catch their breath. 'I'll run next door and get a pot of tea and some cakes,' said Kay. 'Wow, did you see that! Lightning and any minute now ...' Thunder rumbled as Kay laughed and darted out of the door, running the few steps to Lemon's just as the rain came down.

Now the storm had broken it seemed to bring out the full dizzying scent of the violets. Ruan smiled to herself, for one customer had thought they were selling them in small bunches. *Her* violets, from that darling man who at this very moment was busily at work at the Mask, discussing with Buckley and Valentinova the various aspects of tonight's play. Ruan had seen him in costume, a black and dull-silver doublet, worn with narrow black tights that made his legs even more long and raking as he moved about the stage.

The Mask was an attractive theatre, she thought, wincing as another fork of lightning lit the sky. She liked the Roman frontage, with its columns and stone balustrade, rising to a roof with a raised glass dome, which seen from inside was like a diamond-cut bowl from which hung twelve gilt-copper lamps. Other parts of the ceiling were studded with old-gold stars, and the halfmoon circles were decoratively carved. The scarlet curtains of the boxes matched the sweeping drapery of the proscenium arch.

'No other play opens so excitingly as *Hamlet*,' Tarquin had said, his hand gripping hers as they had lingered on after supper at the Mill, the candles slowly guttering on the tables. 'The battlements of Elsinore, and the dusk-light stealing over the castle. The guard, alarmed by the presence he can't see.'

Ruan knew with all her heart that the play would be memorable, from the moment Tarquin walked on-stage to become before her eyes the strange prince, brooding and restless, haunted by a ghost.

Now the rain was pouring down, and the sky had darkened over Avendon. Lightning flashes lit the sudden gloom of the shop, and the thunder shook the windows and made ornaments rattle on their shelves. Ruan decided to switch on the light. Kay was probably waiting until the rain eased off before returning with their tea and cakes.

Ruan reached to the switch, and then with stunning intensity the thunder and lightning cracked and flamed together, lighting up the street outside for one incredible moment. It was as if a bomb had fallen, and Ruan cried out and clapped her hands against her ears. The earth shook, and then everything was still except for the pounding of the rain.

She drew a shaky breath. It must have been a thunderbolt and from the sound of it fairly close to town ... somewhere near the river. She noticed that her hand shook as she switched on the light, and her heart was still hammering. It had been a frightening experience, and through the blurred shop windows she saw that people on the opposite side of the road were coming out of doors, macs over their heads, to gaze curiously in the direction from which the intense flash and the noise had come. She hesitated a moment, suppressed a little shiver, and opened the door of the antique shop.

'Do you think something has been struck, Mr. Lyons?' she called out to the bookseller.

'Aye.' He wore a trilby hat but was otherwise in his shirtsleeves. 'That was a nasty one and I'm betting someone has copped it. Listen, girl! That's the fire brigade!'

The racing bells clanged through another rumble of thunder, and people looked at one another uneasily. The sky was still rather sinister, though the rain had eased. The worst of the storm had passed, but everyone knew that something dreadful had happened up by the river. That bolt from the blue had struck a building and firemen were on their way to the scene of the disaster.

'Ruan!' Kay came running through the fine rain, tea and cakes forgotten, a look of concern on her face. 'My dear, they're saying in Lemon's that the theatre has been struck. The Mask!'

'The Mask?' Ruan gazed at the other girl in stunned disbelief. 'No – it couldn't be. Tarquin's there ... the company are in rehearsal. It couldn't be!'

'Look,' Kay ran into the shop and came out again holding a plastic mac, 'you put this on and run up and see what's happened. You know how these rumours start ... anyway, the lightning might only have struck the outside of the theatre—'

'Not the theatre – please God!' Ruan was trembling as she struggled into the mac. 'M-mind the shop, Kay.'

'Yes, don't worry about the shop ...'

Already Ruan was running in the direction of the theatre, her hair blowing in the wind, the rain on her face ... or was it tears she didn't feel for the fear in her heart?

The grass verge fronting the theatre was alive with spectators, and swarming about the shattered roof of the building itself were firemen, doing something to the stone balustrade that was cracked and scorchmarked, the debris from it littering the pavement below, along with great lumps of glass from the splintered dome.

There was a sudden crash as more of the stonework broke away, followed by the frantic siren of an approaching ambulance. 'Just like the Blitz,' a man muttered. 'They say someone's been badly hurt – poor devil!'

Ruan heard as she thrust her way through the crowd. There was a smell of wet grass, damp raincoats, and brickdust, and something else that reminded her of fireworks. Her acute awareness of all this was mixed in with her frantic desire to get to Tarquin, to see him and hear the blessed sound of his voice. She reached the pavement as the ambulance dashed into sight, and the sight of it, pulling up beyond the cordon around the theatre, was more frightening than anything else had been. It was the symbol of injury and pain, and she stood in silent fear among the shattering groups of onlookers, wanting to dash madly across to the theatre, and yet held back with everyone else by the arm of the law.

'I saw it,' a boy kept saying. 'The sky went dark and this shaft of fire went straight for the dome – straight at it, as if it meant to hit that place and nothing else. I saw it! It smoked, and then came a loud noise and the roof cracked and caved in, and the glass flew about.'

'Please—' Ruan caught at the policeman's arm. 'I have friends in the theatre – can't I go across?'

He looked at her, took in her pale, worried face, and shook his head regretfully. 'I'm sorry, miss. It's dangerous. Part of the roof keeps falling, and everyone has to stand clear until all the rubble is down.'

'Who – who was hurt?' she pleaded.

'I can't say, missie.' He turned his solid back on her, for others in the crowd were pushing forward, excitedly, as if at a sideshow, and had to be restrained as the ambulance men carried someone out of the theatre on a stretcher, the red blanket across the injured person an ominous clash of colour in the grey light of the rain. So still. Unmoving as the stretcher was lifted into the back of the ambulance. Ruan caught her breath as three more people came out of the shattered foyer, stepping over the stonework that lay about. One of them was Buckley Holt, and he was assisting Valentinova to the ambulance. The other person was Ann, looking round dazedly, noticing the crowd, and staring as she caught sight of Ruan in the green plastic mac. She hesitated a few painful seconds, and then came running across the road to where Ruan stood. She was white-faced, shaken, her Ophelia plait a gleam of gold in the rain. She caught at Ruan's hand, and looked pleadingly at the policeman. 'My friend must come with me,' she said. 'It's her fiancé who's been hurt!'

Ruan had known ... perhaps from the moment the lightning had struck. She had felt with her heart and her nerves that a catastrophe had happened in her life, and as the policeman let her pass to walk with Ann to Buckley's car, parked round by the stage entrance and undamaged, she felt as if the ground wavered under her feet. 'Why must it happen to Tarquin?' she wondered bleakly. 'Why must he be the one to suffer when he wouldn't hurt a living thing himself?'

'Ann—?' Her eyes spoke the rest for her.

'It all happened so swiftly.' They stood beside the car, watching as the ambulance sped away, the doors closed against Ruan. 'Quin and Val were down on the aisle, right under the dome with those copper lamps attached. They were studying the stage set for the nunnery scene. Suddenly there was this awful flash, this shattering explosion, and we all went down on all fours, covering our ears as the dome and part of the roof collapsed into the auditorium.'

Ann took a deep breath and tears shone in her eyes. 'Quin is partly the actor he is because of his quick reactions, the way he realizes something ahead of other people. As that flash tore through the theatre he flung himself over Val, protected her as glass, stone and those heavy copper lamps came down on them. Quin – he was caught about the head and the spine. Val was cut and badly shaken up.'

They got into the car in silence and drove away from the shattered theatre, heading in the direction of the hospital. Ruan felt numb with shock, and yet sharply aware of the rain against the windscreen, the heartbeat rhythm of the wiper, and the shine of Ann's knuckles as she gripped the wheel.

Tarquin was very badly hurt. In the midst of the happiness which had prompted him to send her violets; only hours away from his dream of playing Hamlet, he had been struck down by 'the strange impatience of the heavens'.

She sat quiet all through that drive to the hospital, re-membering the way he had smiled in the candlelight last night, with a gay teasing and an underlying gravity. That secret sadness in Tarquin had made her love him all the more ... ah, but she mustn't think of their love as over. He would recover! He would smile again, act again, take her in his arms with his kiss shimmering in his grey eyes before he kissed her lips.

'Don't be too anxious,' Ann said gently, as they parked in the hospital grounds, and she turned a moment to look at Ruan. 'Quin is strong as only a superb actor can be, with amazing resources of vitality. I've seen him play Petruchio with a soaring temperature, and you can imagine how the audience raved over that. He's said ever after that he should always play the part half off his head. Come, let's go inside and find Buck. He'll have talked to a doctor by now and will be able to tell us how severely Quin has been hurt.'

The words sent a shudder through Ruan. It seemed as if she were awake in a nightmare, one that increased in terror as she pictured Tarquin at the mercy of surgical knives. The strength she had often felt in his lean hands was no longer at his command. Unconsciously, now, he lay at the centre of a drama that involved his very life, and hers.

Buck awaited them in the visitors' room. He looked pale and very worried, and had too much respect for Ruan's common sense to put on an act. Valentinova had concussion and was being kept in overnight. Poor Tarquin had caught the brunt of the storm. Standing behind Ruan as he helped her off with her mac, he said quietly: 'They're going to operate on him as soon as possible. They've sent to London for the very best man ... Strathern, the brain surgeon.' Buck's hands tightened on her shoulders as a painful shudder swept her slimness. 'Be brave, honey. Dear old Quin can't be brave for himself just at present, so it's up to us.'

'I know.' She bowed her head and spoke huskily. 'There's a small chapel in the grounds – five years ago my mother lay ill in this hospital – and I'll go and sit there for a little while. I – I suppose none of us can see him?'

Buck shook his head.

'Then I shan't be long.' Ruan walked quietly out of the room and made her way to the mellow little chapel where she used to come and pray that Catrina wouldn't be taken away from her. Its walls on this sad evening took on a strange, beautiful colour, and rain dripped from the tall old fern trees that shaded the path to the oaken door.

She went inside, where there was an air of peace, with white flowers on the altar and a soft speaking light in the eyes of the crucified Christ. Anything could be borne if the love was strong enough. So spoke those eyes as Ruan knelt to pray for the man she so tenderly cared for.

The operation took place at nine o'clock, and it was at midnight when a nurse came to tell them that Mr. Powers had been taken to his room and would remain unconscious throughout the night, and possibly the following day. They were advised to go home, for there was nothing they could do. They could only wait, now, for the surgeon's skill to work its miracle.

'Ruan, come back to the hotel with us,' said Ann. 'You can share my room—'

'You're kind, but I must go home. My stepfather will be wondering what has become of me – I should have telephoned – though if Charme has heard about the accident she'll guess that I've been here, waiting.'

'Are you sure?' Ann looked so anxious. 'Tarquin has said that your stepsister is not a very sympathetic sort—'

'It's best that I go home.'

Ruan wanted to be alone, and at the villa she would be left on her own to brood about Tarquin.

Everything was very quiet when she bade Ann and Buckley goodnight and made her way along Melisande Terrace to the villa. A little rain was falling, obscuring the stars, and her memories were poignant as she turned in at the drive and walked to the steps. She seemed to hear Tarquin laughing in the stillness, gripping her hand as they ran off in their masquerade, eager to be alone together by the river, where today that fearful bolt of lightning had struck him down.

She entered the house and closed the door quietly behind her. When she reached her room and switched on the light she found Taffy dozing on the foot of her bed. He lifted his nose from his paws and his fluffy pom-pom of a tail gave a wag as she walked to the bed and stroked him.

'Waiting up for me, Taff? Do you sense it that tonight there's something amiss with our world?'

The little dog gave a whimper and licked her hand. She hugged him and tears burned in her eyes. His was the only sympathy she could have borne ... not that Charme or her stepfather had bothered to lose any sleep over her.

She carried Taffy to the window seat and he lay on her lap, his presence a comfort as her thoughts dwelt anxiously on that bandaged figure, lying so still in a hospital bed. It was unbearable, for tonight he should have triumphed in the role he had wanted so much to play ... that of Hamlet.

'Goodnight, sweet Prince,' she whispered. 'May you be kept safe through the darkness.'

The following day Ruan was allowed to see Tarquin for just a few minutes. The hospital staff had been told by Buckley Holt that she was the fiancée of the injured actor.

'They'll keep you out otherwise,' Ann whispered. 'Only his nearest is allowed by his bedside ... he has no close relatives, and no one else knows that he has a wife. He needs you, Ruan.'

He had roused a little and the atmosphere in his quiet room was one of hope. A nurse ushered her to his bedside, and behind her reassuring smile there lay a hint of wonder. 'He's such a handsome man,' said the young nurse, and Ruan guessed what she was thinking. Such a man should be engaged to someone madly beautiful. Anxiety had sharpened the contours of her own face, and she was so pale that a kiss would have left a bruise. Her eyes were shadowed from restless sleep, like flowers left out in the rain.

She sat down in the chair beside the bed, knowing she mustn't touch him, though she longed to kiss lightly his lean and hollowed cheek.

Never before had she seen his eyes closed and his face so still. It was not considered the thing to call a man beautiful, but there was in Tarquin's face the aristocratic strength and beauty of fine bones. His lips were moulded as if by the hand of a sculptor. Could she really believe that such a man desired her? Could she hope to hold him ... if when he recovered he took her to Rome, to be with him among smart, worldly people?

Anxiety for him caught her by the throat as her gaze dwelt on the bandages that swathed his head. Hugh Strathern was the best, Ann had said. If anyone could make Tarquin well and strong again it was the rather dour surgeon who not so long ago had gone out with a rescue boat to a small island off the coast of Cornwall, to operate on a young boy who had fallen from the cliffs and who might have died but for the skill that had been so fortunately at hand. The surgeon had been staying with a friend who lived in that part of the country.

And then her heart came into her throat as Tarquin's eyes fluttered open. They gazed straight at her, taking in slowly the russet gleam of her hair against the white paint-work of the room. Dwelling on each feature with a gravity that held no glimmer of recognition, Ruan tried not to be alarmed. The nurse had warned her that it would be several days before Mr. Powers regained full awareness of people and of his own identity. He had sustained a fracture of the skull and though the pressure had now been lifted he was still in a state of severe concussion.

'Hullo, darling,' she whispered, but he just went on looking at her with those empty grey eyes, and then he drifted off to sleep again. The nurse came quietly to the bedside and bent over him. 'They always sleep a lot after an operation,' she assured Ruan. 'Sleep will mend him.'

When Ruan left the hospital she wandered by the river. It was sad to look at the Mask, with tarpaulin stretched across the roof and red-lettered banners across the play-boards to announce that the theatre would be closed while repairs were made to the interior. Until then the company

76

would take a rest. Some of them might return to London, for actors were superstitious. A theatre struck by lightning took on the aspect of an unlucky house.

Ruan was to meet Ann for tea at Lemon's, but first she called in at the shop to see how Kay was managing and to acquaint her with Tarquin's progress. They couldn't talk for long. Leonard Wells was there serving a customer, and Kay whispered that another girl was taking Ruan's place on Monday. 'I didn't know you were leaving,' she added, looking rather hurt. 'You might have told me.'

'I meant to . . .' Ruan remembered with a jolt that all her plans had been geared to going away with Tarquin. Rome had awaited them with its promise of a new life for both of them, but now it might be weeks before Tarquin was fit enough to travel, and in the meantime she was jobless. Well, she had her two weeks' holiday money and a little cash saved up. And it would be nice to be free to go and see Tarquin as often as possible.

'Leonard put your basket of violets out in the yard,' Kay said ruefully. 'All that rain in the night has soaked them.'

'It's all right . . .' Yet Ruan could have wept, for the violets had been so lovely and everything had seemed so unclouded when the boy had come whistling into the shop with them.

'Here's your perfume.' Kay handed it to her with a quick glance at her employer. 'I'm sorry I can't talk more, Ru. All the best, and I do hope Mr. Powers soon gets well.'

'Everyone is very hopeful.' Ruan smiled goodbye at Kay.

'Miss Perry!' Leonard Wells came round to her from his counter and handed her a sealed, buff-coloured envelope. 'I'm sorry you're leaving us. You've always given of your best, and I wish you well in your new position.'

'Thank you, Mr. Wells.' Ruan took the envelope, which she knew contained her stamp-card and her pay cheque, with her fortnight's holiday money added on. 'I've enjoyed working here—'

They both stood hesitant, as if he wished to detain her, as if she half wished he would say the words that would re-employ her.

Then he said, a shade regretfully: 'I've taken on another girl. She's extremely bright and is interested in the antique business.'

'Oh – good.' Ruan smiled. 'I'm sure she'll be just right for you. Goodbye, sir!'

She left quietly, and it was as if a chapter closed in her life. The girl she had been was left behind among the copper ornaments and the porcelain figures. Someone a little older stepped out on to the pavement and walked towards the black and white exterior of Lemon's. Ann awaited her at a corner table, and they shared a pot of tea and ate thinly cut anchovy sandwiches without much appetite. Until Tarquin was quite out of danger they would be anxious, rather listless. Then catching each other's eye they forced themselves to smile and talk of other things.

'Buck is working on the designs for a play to be produced at the Shaftesbury in October,' said Ann. 'It's a mod production of a Greek drama I acted with Tarquin at the Herod Atticus Theatre in Athens. It's a wonderful place, with a great basin of stone seats and a wide, open-air stage with a background of arches all tawny with age. The acoustics are marvellous. Tarquin would stand at the centre of the stage and let his voice ring to the very last rim of seats. *"Go tell the king: The laurels are cut down; the fair-wrought halls have fallen to the ground."* '

Ann smiled a little sadly. 'Almost prophetic, those words when you come to think of it.'

'Greece must be a wonderful country.' Ruan was pushing a pastry around her plate with a restless hand. Greece, Rome, the world at large. These places were Tarquin's arena, and she felt suddenly that she would never see their reality. They were a dream, as perhaps Tarquin's love was. What if he had forgotten her for good, the girl from Avendon, so innocently ardent, touching the fringes of the life he shared so actively with people such as Ann and Buckley?

'Athens,' said Ann, 'apart from the temple ruins and the classical drama is the noisiest place on earth. We loved the acting, the *bouzouki* music played in the *tavernas*, and the dancing, but we weren't sorry to get away from the traffic and the blaring motor horns. London is peaceful by comparison. We stage people love the limelight, but there are times when we'd give our souls for a little peace.'

'What happens when the novelty of being peaceful wears off?' Ruan smiled, but there was a nervous quiver to her lips. It was as if Ann had revealed unconsciously what it was in Ruan that Tarquin had turned to.

'We dash back madly to the bright lights, like a lot of giddy moths.' Ann broke into a smile, and then gazed solemnly at Ruan. 'You look so worried, my pet – all eyes and heart. He'll get well, I just know it. He's a fighter, is Quin, of the stuff that the Arran islanders are made, strong-souled, with much to do before his star sets. Ruan, you mustn't fret.' Ann patted her hand, and fingered the blue scarab ring with its shining wings. 'From Quin?'

'Yes. It's a friendship ring.'

'Friendship?' Ann looked teasing. 'You're far too humble, my dear. You'd make a poor actress. My outlook on love is that it's to be enjoyed, not treated as if a man does a girl a great honour by wanting to love her. I get the impression that you're rather afraid of what's between you and Quin. He's only a mortal man, you know. He looks like Apollo, but when Zeus hurled the thunderbolt he couldn't deflect it.'

'His nurse looked at me so oddly,' Ruan's eyes met Ann's, a tiny smile in them. 'I think I shocked her sense of propriety by not looking the picture of glamour.'

'Quin sees all the glamour he needs,' Ann rejoined. 'He's a rather serious person at heart – and then there's Nina, so pretty it must hurt him, and unable to share his life. Her people had no right to let her marry him. They must have known she had a nervous illness and that it could get worse.'

'Perhaps they hoped that marriage would cure her.'

'Marriage with an ambitious young actor? He was going places from the moment he stepped on a stage. It was sheer bad luck that he should meet the girl and be so dazzled by

79

her that he couldn't see that she was all wrong for him. Strange about Quin. His public life has been faultless, but in his private life he's been so unlucky. You could be so good for him, Ruan.'

'What if by loving him I brought down the coals of fire on his head?' Ruan asked gravely. 'He belongs to Nina. Nothing can alter that. I am the interloper.'

'You're too introspective,' Ann argued. 'You mustn't let yourself believe that you're unlucky for him. He needs someone like you.'

'I . . . I don't know.' Ruan touched with her fingertips the scarab ring she had been so wary of taking from him. 'Today at the hospital he didn't know me at all. He looked at me as if I were a stranger.'

'For a time we might all be strangers to him. You must be prepared for that, Ruan. Tell me,' Ann studied her slender face with its winged eyebrows and too-sensitive mouth, 'how old are you? I don't mean to sound nosey, but Buck thinks you're about seventeen.'

'Oh no.' Ruan gave a laugh. 'I shall be twenty in September. My mother always said that I was born with the harvest moon. She said it was huge the night I arrived, that I hopped off it.'

'Quin calls you Pierrette, doesn't he?'

Ruan smiled her agreement. 'Do you think I behave as if I were seventeen? I've often thought of myself as being a bit square. I mean, I don't go for pop music or pop idols. I find all that terribly juvenile.'

'You look so young, so untouched,' Ann mused. 'That look of eternal youth will one day make your husband appear a cradle-snatcher.'

'My – husband?' Ruan's gaze drifted past Ann to the window beside their table, and it was a relief when other members of the Mask company came into the restaurant, spotted Ann and came over to inquire after Tarquin, and to talk with animation about the stricken theatre and their plans for the rest of the season.

Ruan listened for a while, and then feeling an onlooker

rather than a participant, she slipped away and none of the group noticed that she had gone. Even Ann was absorbed in the theatre talk. It was for these people the breath of life. They lived for the raising of the first curtain and the drama of the play.

Ruan walked slowly home, and later when she telephoned the hospital she was told that Mr. Powers was comfortable and making satisfactory progress. It was all so cool and clinical, and a bleak little light came into her eyes.

'Thank you.' She turned from the phone to find Charme looking at her from the staircase. Her stepsister was on the way out to an appointment. She wore a cream suit with a soft ring of fawn-coloured fur around the deep collar. Her heels were high, her nylons sheer, her gaze inquisitive.

'I've heard a funny rumour,' she said casually. 'Simon got it from a reporter on the *Avendon Herald*. It seems that your Tarquin Powers is a married man – did you know, sweetie, or has he been keeping you in the dark?'

'Yes, I knew,' said Ruan with a sigh. By tomorrow the news would be all over Avendon, and she shrank from the tag 'the other woman' which would be hung around her neck.

'You are your mother's daughter, aren't you?' drawled Charme. 'Soft-hearted and ready to be taken in by the first good-looking man who comes your way. I hope, my dear, that you took heed of what I said to you the other evening. Father and I want no scandal on our doorstep.'

'Don't worry!' Ruan drew herself up very straight, a willow of a girl, with the sunset light in her russet hair making it burn around her pale young face. 'I intend to move out right away. I can get a room at the Bard and Harp – tell your father that he has always been as kind to me as you would allow.'

Charme slowly raised an eyebrow, and then with a cool self-containment she walked to the front door. 'Please yourself! You're no infant or that actor wouldn't want you. I'll say this much for you, Ruan, you have the courage of your foolishness. Don't you know that Father and I could have arranged a much more suitable match for you?'

Ruan stared at Charme and her heart began to thump in the most alarming fashion. 'Who – who are you talking about?'

'You met him, my pet. He's been abroad for many years and has got out of touch with the people he knew, the girls he might have courted, and now that he has settled down in a house of his own he wants someone to share it with him.'

'You can't mean Eduard Talgarth?'

'Why not?'

'But I thought—'

'What did you think? That I was going to give up Simon to run a large old mansion down in Cornwall? Not on your life! As I told Eduard, you're the type for cliffs and coves and a draughty chateau. I believe he agreed with me, and he might have proposed if you hadn't shown him so plainly that you thought him unattractive.'

'I ... I disliked his arrogance.' Ruan was shocked by the mere idea of being proposed to by that dark, piratical man from Cornwall. If she had known what the St. Cyrs had in mind she would have left their house several weeks ago. They had actually thought of handing her over to that bold stranger as if she were a bale of goods he might have carried on one of those island-hopping ships of his!

'I'm glad he left Avendon,' she exclaimed.

'No man likes to be shown by a girl that she finds him hateful. I thought he had a certain rugged charm, but a man who wants to live in the wilds, with the sea pounding at his door, is not my glass of champagne.' Charme flicked her hazel-gold eyes over her young stepsister. 'What puzzles me is what you've got. Is it something fey and Celtic for older men only? None of my boy-friends ever found you pretty, though your hair isn't a bad colour, if you'd only have such a mane cut and styled.'

'It suits me.' Ruan tossed back the russet mane with a defiant movement of her head, and the flash to her eyes made Charme look at her with sharp curiosity.

'And the actor, presumably. Is he separated from his

wife?'

'No – she happens to be an invalid.'

'Oh, I see.'

'No, Charme, you don't see anything. Tarquin and I like each other, but there has never been a love affair.'

'You were his muse, eh, until the lightning struck. What now, Ruan? Personally speaking I think you'd do better to think about a husband rather than a married boy-friend.'

'Someone like Eduard Talgarth, who thinks love can be bought?'

'The gilt wears off romance quicker than it wears off a bonded security,' Charme drawled. 'We might have been friends, you and I, if you had never been such a dreamer, like a character in a Lewis Carroll book who can't come down to earth. You're like Alice who wandered through the looking glass and found herself at a party where everyone talked of things she couldn't understand. In the end she ran away!'

The door snapped shut. Charme had gone, but her words lingered in the hall with her perfume.

'In the end she ran away . . . ran away . . .'

CHAPTER FIVE

A SINGLE light burned, otherwise the hospital room was very still. All that day Tarquin had been very low, and Ruan had waited for hours, her every nerve tensed for a footfall, some word that he had rallied again. It was awful to be powerless to do anything but wait, but when accident struck only those of science could help; those who cared could only keep a lonely vigil. Ann and her fiancé were not present this evening; they had gone to London to visit Buck's parents.

'Miss Perry!'

Ruan got to her feet and gazed anxiously at the large figure of Hugh Strathern, all shoulders and a noble head of red hair, but his hands were as fine-boned as a woman's. He came to her and laid those hands on her shoulders.

'You're always here, aren't you, standing by. Well, come with me, young lady, and let's see if your voice can reach that young man. Science can do everything but play the role of woman – do you understand me?'

'Yes.' She understood that at last she was wanted.

All through the night Ruan sat and talked to Tarquin, of the things of childhood and school; the funny and the sad, half-forgotten and now remembered. Her voice made a soft sound in the quiet room as she talked of the plays she had seen him in, and he lay very still, clinging to the awareness of sound, the feminine softness of her voice. Life, love, a woman at his bedside . . . but when at last he murmured a name, it was Nina.

As the morning light drifted into the room and the night lamp was extinguished, Hugh Strathern looked at his patient and nodded to himself. Then he took hold of Ruan and took her from the room.

'The lad is sleeping. Come and drink coffee with me, and then you can go home and sleep.'

'You mean—?' She gazed at him with hopeful eyes.

He nodded. 'I've seen it before. Men can't be born without a woman, and they don't want to die if a woman cares enough to hold them back. He'll be all right now. It was a kind of crisis, and he needed to know that a certain woman was with him.'

'Me?' she asked wistfully, remembering how he had murmured a name that was not hers.

Strathern shook his red head. 'Nina, his wife. He probably blames himself in part for her illness, and last night he believed she was with him. He rallied because of her, not you. D'you understand, my girl?'

'Not fully.' She gazed over her coffee cup at the surgeon. 'Do tell me everything. I want to understand.'

'Right!' Three spoonfuls of sugar went into the surgeon's cup of black coffee. 'Powers has suffered a skull fracture induced by lightning and thunder. They're supernatural things – part of the plays he's often acted in. Ever seen him as Cassius?'

She nodded, a light in her eyes.

'Magnificent portrayal. No other actor gets the character as right as he does – Iscariot – Betrayal – Love – Hatred. Actors are strange people, young woman. They live their parts, on and off the stage. Now take this business of Nina, his wife. He loved her, perhaps he still loves her, but there are times when he wishes her out of his life. This sets up a guilt barrier, and he was at that barrier last night. He had to find Nina – she had to come to him – and so I put you at his bedside. He thought you Nina, my child. And now there is every chance that when he recovers fully he will have forgotten who you are, and what you meant to him.'

Ruan's heart beat heavily. She was both tired and strung to a pitch of acute awareness. 'You mean that because of this haunting feeling of guilt, he has now put me out of his life?'

'It's something you must be prepared for,' Strathern warned.

'Last night I was his safeguard because he thought me

85

Nina. Now you are saying—' But she couldn't put it into words. It was too much to take. It was too painful.

'If he doesn't know you when he sees you,' said Hugh Strathern, 'then there's little hope that he will remember that he loved you. You've been part of his guilt, now he has slipped free of that guilt, and if there is continued non-acceptance of you – as Ruan – then don't stay around to torment yourself, my child.'

'What will I do?' she asked bleakly. 'Where shall I go? We had planned, Tarquin and I, to be together in Rome.'

'Would you have been truly happy?' asked the blunt surgeon.

She hesitated, for something about the man's honesty compelled the painful truth. She shook her head. 'I love him, that's all I know for sure.'

'If he knows you, then you'll go away with him?'

'Yes – if he wants me.' She met the surgeon's eyes, a blue-green, rather like a balmy sea. 'You think it would be wrong, and that in the end Nina would come between us?'

'Inevitably. I've been in touch with the clinic at Los Angeles. It isn't that she can recover ... it's that she can't that will finally make his guilt intolerable for you.'

Ruan couldn't speak. He was too wise, this man, not to be telling her the blunt facts.

'You're young,' he said. 'Go seek another place to live, another love to help you forget.'

'Where do you suggest?' Her smile was fleeting. 'Land's End?'

'H'm, right now you need some sleep,' he said gruffly. 'Go home and rest, and perhaps I shall think of something for you to do.'

'You, Mr. Strathern?'

'Me, young woman. This crusty, elderly cynic, who was once much in love himself. We were married, Sheila and I, but I lost her when our daughter was born.'

'I ... I had no idea,' Ruan said with sympathy. 'I'm sorry.'

'I don't talk about it. Yseult is at school – the convent

86

sort over in France – and in two weeks she'll come home for the summer holidays. She's a mite delicate. I'd like her to have a long holiday by the sea. Maybe—'

'Maybe what, Mr. Strathern?'

'Well, we'll wait a bit. See what develops.'

'No, please go on, now you've gone this far!'

'Well, I was thinking that I'd need someone to be with Yseult – I'm tied by my work, you understand. One of the teachers is bringing her over from Brittany – I thought you could meet her, and perhaps spend the summer with her.'

'You – you seem very certain that I'll be at a loose end.'

He shrugged his broad shoulders. 'Brain surgery is my business. Has Powers shown any signs yet that he remembers you?'

'No.' The word emerged as a pained whisper.

'I'm sorry, child. But in the long run it could be for the best.'

'No matter how much it hurts?'

'There's always pain when something needs mending.'

'My foolish heart?'

'You're still in your teens, Ruan Perry. And you've grit. You sat by that bedside last night and talked when it would have been easier to weep. He's quite a man, eh, lass? Handsome as one of those Greek gods mentioned in books?'

She nodded. 'And kind. That's why it worries him to be happy when Nina can't be. It's been a sad marriage. He's deserved better – warmth, companionship, children. He's more than a gifted actor, Mr. Strathern.'

'You wouldn't love him if he were less.' The blue-green eyes dwelt shrewdly upon her. 'If things don't work out for you, will you be a companion for my girl while she's home for the summertime? Yseult is a nice creature – imaginative. Your sort. But it worries me that she has her mother's delicate constitution and not mine. Bull Strathern, they used to call me at medical college.'

'You have a soft heart,' Ruan smiled.

'Aye, soft for those I like, and I like genuine people.'

They parted on those words, and Ruan walked home

through the early morning sunshine to the Tudor inn where she had been staying for the past week. St. Cyr had turned up and tried to persuade her to return to the villa, but she had been adamant. There was no more room for her in their lives and she had chosen to go her own way. The room she had booked at the Bard and Harp was a temporary arrangement. She might go and work in London, where she would find more permanent accommodation.

She gazed around at the well-known town in which she had lived for twelve years, and she knew it would be a wrench to leave Avendon. It was an attractive place, but she felt she could no longer stay here – not if Tarquin had forgotten their days on the river, and the love he had vowed.

She tilted her chin bravely. Strathern had warned her very clearly that she might no longer mean anything to Tarquin. In which event she would really be on her own, to choose between London, or a summer job as companion to the young daughter of the man who had saved Tarquin. Every moment they had shared was precious, and something to be always grateful for. He might so easily have died, and that would have been infinitely harder to bear.

Ruan visited the hospital regularly, but upon Strathern's advice she didn't go in to see Tarquin. They must wait and see if he asked for her.

He didn't.

He never mentioned her to Ann, or showed any sign that he had been in love with a girl while starring in plays at the Mask. He remembered the theatre. Knew all the company and every play, right up to the moment when the lightning struck. He spoke vividly of being in the aisle with Valentinova when the dome had cracked and caved in on them. He was clear on every point but one ... when Ann mentioned casually a girl called Ruan, he asked if she were a member of the cast. 'Though I can't recall the name,' he added.

It was over!

Ruan knew it before she received an invitation from

Hugh Strathern to have a meal with him at the Mill Loft. She dressed herself attractively and applied colour to lips set in a plucky smile. No one must know how deep was the hurt that she was the one person Tarquin could not recall. She who loved him had become a stranger to him, shut out of his memories, and his life.

She had to learn how to live without him, and she was ready to be swayed by the blunt, shrewd surgeon who had mentioned already a plan that would make it easy for her to slip out of Avendon.

She had only ever seen him in a flying white coat, and this evening he wore olive-green tweeds and his thick red hair was brushed smooth. 'You look nice, lass,' he said with appreciation. 'I feel fifteen years younger, taking supper with a pretty girl. Now what will you have to drink? I'm a gin and tonic man. Find it peps me up after a busy day.'

'I'll have the same,' she said. 'It was nice of you, Mr. Strathern, to drive all the way down from London to see me.'

'I count it a pleasure.' He turned to the waiter to order their drinks, and then he sat looking at her, a shrewd light in his sea-green eyes. 'You haven't cried once, have you? It might help.'

'I'm not the weeping sort.' She forced the smile back to her lips. 'And I don't regret knowing Tarquin, and loving him. But I won't pretend that he'll be easy to forget. Unlike me he isn't the forgettable sort.'

'You mustn't believe that what he felt for you was fleeting and casual. On the contrary, child, it's the deep-felt things that sometimes have to be pushed into hiding or they might drive us mad.'

'Then you think – in time—?' She looked both wistful and eager, her eyes grey-violet, shadowed by the lashes that gave her a look that hinted at Celtic mysteries.

'He might one day remember you, Ruan, but you must accept for the present that you're a stranger to him. Have you thought over my suggestion, that you spend the summer with Yseult and keep an eye on her for me?'

She hesitated to speak as the waiter brought their drinks and asked if they would like to order their meal. They both decided on chilled melon to start, with a steak and salad for Strathern, and a chicken and mushroom omelette for Ruan. They were then alone again and he was looking at her, waiting for her answer.

'I ... I had thought of going to London,' she said. 'I must find a regular job.'

'But surely you intend to take a holiday?'

'These past two weeks were my holiday.'

'It has hardly been a fortnight of relaxation. Look, Ruan, I really need someone to look after my girl for the summer. I'm not suggesting the arrangement out of a sense of pity. God forbid! Being proud myself I can see what sort of a girl you are.' The ice rattled in his glass as he lifted it to his lips. His eyes held hers over the rim. 'It would be *congé payé*. Six weeks by the sea, and the undemanding friendship of my Yseult. Otherwise I shall have to find someone else for the job – some staid woman, no doubt, who wouldn't be such fun for Yseult to be with.'

'You're very persuasive, Mr. Strathern.' Ruan smiled a little as she took a sip of her drink and felt the ice cool against her lips. It was a rather lovely evening, with the long red shadows of sunset stretching across the fields and touching the watermill to tawny beauty.

'I think you want to be persuaded,' he said bluntly. 'London is a noisy, bustling place, and a stranger to it can feel devilish lonely. Some time in the country will rest you, and prepare you for the city. Being with my youngster might help you to forget the anxiety of these past two weeks. Might make more bearable the heartache you're feeling right now.'

'Do you think Yseult would like me?'

'She's my daughter, Ruan, and I like you. Ah, here comes our supper. I'm ravenous! Had a particularly interesting case to deal with, but I'd better not talk shop. I'm forgetting you aren't one of my nurses.' He glanced up from his melon on ice. 'Have you ever thought of taking up nursing?'

'I've too much imagination,' she smiled. 'Antiques are more my line. Inanimate things that can't feel pain if they happen to get broken.'

'You're very vulnerable, Ruan, child.' He looked directly into her eyes. 'You need someone strong to take care of you. Someone not like that actor man; older, less romantic, more down to earth.'

She shook her head. 'I don't want to fall in love again. It's so wonderful, and then it's over and you're more aware of loneliness than ever before. This is nice melon.'

'Mmmm, lovely and sweet.'

'It should be,' her dimple came and went as she looked at the crusting of brown sugar he had given the melon on his plate.

'You should smile more often, Ruan. That's quite a dimple you have.'

'It's odd. It has no twin,' she rejoined. She wanted to forget that once in a dream she had been asked if it was for pepper or spice. That later on it had held kisses from Tarquin.

'Where will Yseult be spending her holiday?' she asked.

'Ah, in a very lovely and legendary place.' His eyes lit up. 'I have a house there — or rather it's two cottages knocked into one, with a modernized interior, but with the exterior kept intact. You know, time-mellowed stone walls, and a thick tawny thatching. I bought the place a couple of years ago, and now and again I go there for a bit of a rest. I take out my boat, the *Saucy Bride*, and do some fishing. I have a friend who lives only a few miles from the cottage. Makes it sort of cosy — if you can call such a wild and wonderful place by that term!'

Ruan stared across the table at Hugh Strathern and remembered the boy who had fallen from some high cliffs and been operated on by the surgeon, who happened to be staying in the district.

'You're talking about Cornwall!' she exclaimed.

'That I am, lass. There's no place like it. The land of King Arthur and his Knights. Where the sea folk still believe in the legend of the mermaid, and where the moorland dwellers walk quick across the heather when the sun sets. They say the stone people still dance, and you might hear a footfall on the bracken right behind you.'

Hugh Strathern cut into his steak with appetite. 'Yes, Cornwall. Yseult loves the place. Last year a cousin of mine was able to stay with her at the cottage, but she's since got married and I'm left in a spot.' He glanced up at Ruan. 'You'd find Cornwall much to your liking. It's the perfect place for someone with a lot of imagination, and the bathing can't be bettered – superb beaches, majestic cliffs, and old castle ruins for you and the child to explore. Come, can you resist my sales talk?'

She met his smile, but her thoughts were confused. Cornwall was a big place, but when you didn't care to run into someone a place could become awfully small. You could expect at any moment to come face to face with the one person you wished to avoid. That person was Eduard Talgarth. She wanted never again to meet the man who thought of love as something to be bought.

'I don't know what to do,' she confessed. 'I keep hoping that Tarquin will remember me, and if I go away—'

'Look,' said Strathern, 'I'll strike a bargain with you. See him tomorrow. Confront him now he's on the mend, see him with that attractive actress, and if he knows you, then forget I ever mentioned Cornwall. On the other hand,' Strathern pursed his lips, 'if you find that you mean no more to him, then do what I ask. Go to Cornwall and meet the boat that will be bringing Yseult home from Brittany. Go with her to the cottage and spend the summer there.'

'You're making it an ultimatum?' she half smiled.

'I am, lass. Someone has to make up your mind for you. Now is it a bargain?'

She fiddled with the salt pot, and the ring on her hand was a sparkling blue in the dim, romantic light of the Mill. Strathern put out his hand and touched it. 'Unusual ring. It looks like a flying beetle with gemmed wings.'

'It's a scarab. Tarquin gave it to me. It's a symbol of

protection, and is supposed to bring good fortune.'

'You feel very much hurt, don't you, lass?' Strathern spoke with a gentleness that would have amazed his medical colleagues, who knew him as a blunt, brilliant man with little time for women, except as patients who needed his skill. He was reputed to have loved only one woman.

'Yes.' Ruan felt instinctively the kindness beneath his rugged exterior. She could open her heart to him when even with Ann she was reserved, quiet about the extent of her despair. It seemed as if happiness itself had been taken from her. 'He said such lovely things to me. He said he needed me. Now I am the one person he seems to have forgotten, as if I never counted.'

'I've told you, lass, at present for Tarquin Powers you are easier to forget than to remember. He feels torn by guilt because he loves you instead of that poor, nerve-torn creature miles away in Los Angeles. He's a sensitive man, otherwise he'd take you for his own without a scruple. He'd say what other men would say. Nina can't give me love and affection, but Ruan can.'

Tears came into her eyes as Strathern spoke, for how could she forget those perfect days on the river, when each thing they said, each glance they exchanged, had held the excitement of their growing love. He was in her heart, a tenderness and a tempest.

'Tomorrow you will go and see him,' said Strathern. 'It will hurt even more if he looks at you with a stranger's eyes, but there is a remedy.'

'Cornwall?' she murmured.

'Aye, an escape to the sun, Ruan. A chance for you to forget, or for him to remember.' He lifted his wine glass to his lips and took a deliberate sip. 'Your eyes ask me when you must go. It will be next weekend. Yseult is coming home a little earlier than the other pupils because she has had a bad cold and I want her to get some good Cornish air into her lungs as soon as possible.'

He paused and a gruffness came into his voice. 'I don't want anything to happen to the youngster. She's all I've got, apart from my work.'

Ruan was moved by his words. To have someone was not to be alone. Loneliness was so unbearable.

For the remainder of the evening they talked of other things, and it was around ten o'clock when he escorted her to the Bard and Harp. 'Drive home carefully, Mr. Strathern,' she said.

'It would be nice if you'd call me Hugh, though I admit it's a rather villainous name.' He smiled. 'My wife used to tease me about it.'

'Yseult never knew her?' Ruan murmured.

'No, more's the pity. It has always been my regret that Sheila died young and that Yseult was deprived of knowing her. I try to spend as much time as possible with the girl, but as you can understand I'm kept fairly busy. I only wish I could get away before August. Ruan—?'

'Very well,' she committed herself. 'I'll be Yseult's holiday companion – if Tarquin doesn't want me.'

'Good girl!' He pressed her hand, and then slid behind the wheel of his car. '*Au revoir*, my lass. You have my phone number, so keep in touch with me.'

'I will. Goodnight, Hugh.'

He flashed her a smile, and then he was gone, leaving her alone beneath the wind-swayed signboard of the inn. *Au revoir*. The words echoed through her mind. Would she and Tarquin meet again . . . to love again?

It was early in the morning when Ruan left Avendon. With a gallant tilt to her chin she took a bus to the railway station. 'Off on a holiday?' remarked the conductor, taking note of her suitcase.

'Yes.' She kept on smiling because she didn't dare to stop. 'I'm going to Cornwall.'

'Lucky you! They say it's better than going abroad. My wife wants to visit Italy. She wants to see the fountain of Trevi. Seems to imagine she's going to toss in a coin and meet that Latin heartbreaker who was in that film all about Rome. You women!' he laughed. 'Aren't you a romantic lot?'

'I suppose we are,' Ruan agreed.

She was on her way to London, to see a little of it with Hugh Strathern and to buy clothes suitable for a beach holiday. She would leave on Friday for Pencarne, to open the cottage, air the bed linen, and buy supplies of food. The boat bringing Yseult home would arrive on Sunday, giving Ruan a little time to get accustomed to the cottage and its picturesque surroundings.

She was met at the station by Hugh, who didn't waste time on sympathetic remarks. What more could be said, what use were words, how could they console her? She and Tarquin had met as planned, but seeing her had made no difference to the lapse of memory which made her a stranger to him. He had not known her for the girl he had fallen in love with.

Strathern drove her to a small hotel where she booked in for three days, then with a smile he told her that he was going to show her London in one fell swoop ... this turned out to be lunch at the G.P.O. tower, which reared its strange shape into the sky above historic Fitzroy Square. An express lift swooped them to the sky lounge, where he ordered drinks and showed her a letter from Yseult, who was thrilled that her Pops had found her a nice young companion for the summertime. She looked forward immensely to showing Ruan all over romantic Cornwall. They would visit Tintagel, and Dozemare Pool on the moors. And they mustn't miss going to St. Avrell.

Ruan glanced at Strathern. 'Is the cottage anywhere near St. Avrell?' she asked, for the name had a significance she couldn't dismiss. It was there that Charme's merchant prince had his chateau!

'St. Avrell is about five miles from Pencarne.' Hugh's eyes searched her face, which revealed some of her dismay. 'There are sheer cliffs, high breakers, a lonely sort of grandeur that cuts it off the map for the ordinary tourist looking for a suntan and souvenir shops. You seem to have heard of it – perhaps in connection with the case of the girl who was discovered in one of the coves, a local beauty, found strangled by her own long dark hair.'

Ruan caught her breath. It seemed as if there had to be something dramatic about the place where Eduard Talgarth lived, master of a house built long ago for a French noble. There had to be a rugged grandeur, dangerous seas, and a girl left strangled by her lover.

'Looking forward to this holiday?' Strathern spoke rather wistfully, as if he wished to run away to Cornwall with Ruan and his schoolgirl daughter.

'Yes, I think I am.' She leaned forward to gaze from the windows of the revolving lounge high over London. Hugh pointed out places of interest, and she forced herself to be attentive. She must look forward now, and try to forget the polite smile of the stranger which Tarquin had given her when she had said goodbye to him. Her only consolation was that he had looked so much better, and could move the long legs which might so easily have been handicapped. His spine was terribly bruised, but X-rays had revealed no permanent damage.

He would stride again across a stage. He would go to Rome, and might never remember that she was the girl to whom he had said: 'Come with me. I can't be alone any more.'

After lunch, Hugh took Ruan out on to the windswept terrace of the tower, and as her hair whipped his cheek she said breathlessly that it was like the high poop deck of a sailing ship. His hand gently nipped her waist. 'You're full of imagination,' he said. 'Yseult will like that. She's of your breed, Ruan – romantic, idealistic, swept by compassions that seem foolish to harder folk. You and she are the fable folk. You need protecting.'

'Oh, I don't know,' she smiled. 'I've stood square on my own feet since my mother died. My stepfather couldn't really be bothered with me, and Charme has never known what to make of someone who prefers messing about on the river to sitting under a drier in a hairdresser's. I've had to be independent, and I think I've coped quite well.'

'You've coped splendidly,' he agreed, 'but you've been lonely, haven't you, lass? Maybe that was why you fell so in love—'

'No,' she shook her head. 'Loving Tarquin was not on the rebound from loneliness. It had a magic quality. It was something that happened as if we were spellbound. I don't think I shall ever forget him.'

'Then you'll condemn yourself to future loneliness, Ruan.'

'Can't a woman, or a man, find something other than love to take the place of being lonely?' She met the surgeon's eyes. 'Haven't you?'

'My work is important, to me and to others, but—' he shrugged his shoulders, 'at the end of the day I go home to well-ordered rooms, and I eat alone a meal prepared by my housekeeper. I read, watch a little television – I enjoy those old Hollywood movies scorned by the with-it brigade – and I have a few golfing cronies. No, Ruan! There's little else that can take the place of a loving companion.'

'Then we're a pair!' She smiled with an innocence unassumed. 'We've loved and lost. Hugh, it was good of you to bring me here to this fascinating place. One must be able to see all over London.'

'There are several more places we must see together, before you leave on Friday for Cornwall. Have you seen much of London?'

'Not a lot. Before Catrina died we lived at Warwick where she worked for a rather crotchety lady writer. Stephen St. Cyr came there one day to discuss the buying of some land owned by Naomi Kane, saw my mother and fell in love with her. I think she married him more for my sake than her own. She wanted security and was afraid that if she died while I was still a child I'd be put into an orphanage. But I'm afraid I was always a misfit in the St. Cyr household. The only real happiness came with Tarquin . . .'

Ruan turned and smiled at Hugh Strathern. 'I'm not sad,' she assured him. 'Only very glad that you were his surgeon and that he'll get well and strong again. He has much to give the world, and I think I always knew that our time together was too lovely, too like a dream to last beyond the time allowed for dreaming.'

There was a little silence, as if Strathern was very moved. And then he said gruffly: 'I'm glad my Yseult will have your company through the summertime. I'm glad you will have hers. It's a good arrangement.'

'I'm happy with it,' Ruan said brightly.

'Aye, a little happier than you were.' He took her by the arm and they left the high terrace of the tower. He paid the bill and they stood waiting to go down in the lift. A young couple stood nearby holding hands, and Ruan had to glance away. She couldn't help but remember the man with a whimsical, teasing light in his eyes who used to hold her hand, pressing into her bones, but gently, the ring with the blue scarab ... the ring he had first put on her left hand and which she had wrenched off, thinking he mocked her.

She would go on remembering vividly all they had said, all the little meanings attached to love. He had forgotten, and might never remember again the girl he had called 'dear nymph'.

In the next couple of days Ruan saw Hugh Strathern whenever he was free, and they explored the London he loved – Parliament Square, so wonderfully gothic, with its clock tower crowned by a steeple that looked lacy against the blue sky. They walked across the squares dappled by leaf shadows, the bright red buses passing by, the turrets and pinnacles old-gold with age.

They stood on Tower Bridge and gazed down upon the broad, silky waters of the Thames. The Tower stood massive, indestructible, black and grey in the sunlight. Here long ago the royal barges had set out for the other palaces along the river, now the riverbanks were lined with mysterious-looking warehouses, and a merchant ship stood at anchor, its funnels dark with smoke and sea weather. She was called the *Lady Erline* and men were busy unloading her cargo.

'Have you ever wanted to set sail for far places?' Ruan smiled. 'To see spice islands and seven-storey pagodas?'

'Have you, my lass?'

'Oh, I'm just a dreamer really. I expect if one saw those places in reality they wouldn't be half as exotic as we imagine them. I wonder where that old ship has been and what she carries below her decks?'

'Something quite ordinary, I expect. Crates of rum or sacks of sugar.'

'Not silks and perfumes and smuggled pearls?'

Hugh studied her with an odd smile. 'You seem very interested in that kind of trading, which still goes on in certain parts of the East.'

'Yes, I gathered as much from someone I once met – a man who was interested in my stepsister. I'm sure he was a pirate of the high seas!' She gave a laugh. 'Hugh, do you think me as young and romantic as Yseult?'

'In some ways you're young. In others—' He laid his hand over hers on the sun-warmed rail of the bridge. 'Your name suits you well, Ruan. You attract and yet you're elusive as running water. Well, lass, where shall we go and eat?'

'You choose.' She slipped her hand from his and lifted it to smooth her hair. There must be no flirting with Hugh. He was a rather lonely man and ready to like her beyond friendship, and she didn't wish to hurt him. He was someone who deserved better than love on the rebound.

He took her to the Square Rigger in the heart of the city, a pub designed to look like the inside of a ship, and over their meal she talked of all the impersonal things she could think of. Tomorrow she would be leaving for Cornwall, and Hugh would soon become immersed again in his important work. He would soon forget that for a few days he had thought of her romantically, and away from him she would not feel this treacherous need to turn to him for comfort.

It was over this last lunch together that she decided to take the midnight train to Cornwall, and he phoned Paddington Station and booked her a sleeper. He then drove her to the hotel, where in the lounge they said *au revoir*.

'I shall be coming down in about a month,' he said. 'The keys to the cottage are with Mrs Lovibond, who looks after the place for me. She and her son, who's a fisherman, live just down the hillside so you won't feel too cut off from people. I've also been in touch with the manager of the Pencarne bank and there'll be ample money on deposit for you and Yseult. Now is there anything we've forgotten?'

'I don't think so. I meet the steamer from Brittany on Sunday morning and Yseult will then be put in my charge by the teacher who is bringing her home.'

'Aye, the teacher is taking leave on account of her sister's illness in a Devon nunnery. Sister Grace will be clad in the robe and wimple, so you'll have no trouble identifying her pupil.'

'I bet Yseult has your hair,' Ruan smiled.

He smiled in return. 'Aye, I plead guilty to branding the child with the foxfire, however she looks like her mother in all other respects, and it worries me – ah, but I'm sure this summer will work wonders. You'll see to it that she gets plenty of sea air and sunshine, and plenty of good Cornish cream.'

'I'll be her big sister in every way,' Ruan assured him. 'I'm used to boats, so have I your permission to take her—'

'No!' The word broke sharply from him. 'Not the two of you alone! Jem Lovibond will take you sailing in the *Saucy Bride*. The Cornish waters along that part of the coast are too wild and capricious for a girl to cope with. Always go out with Jem. I insist on that.'

'Of course.' She pressed his arm to reassure him, the parent of an only child, afraid of losing what he loved. 'I promise to do whatever you ask of me with regard to Yseult. What of the moors, Hugh? I've heard there are bogs.'

'Yseult will know them, but they're infrequent around Pencarne. It's up near St. Avrell that you have to beware of running into one, especially on a misty day.'

'We won't be going there – at least, no more than once if

Yseult wants to visit the place.' Ruan spoke tensely, for she had no wish to run into Eduard Talgarth. But it was strange ... so very strange that he should have said that she would visit his part of the world, where the heather grew high enough to hide a girl. It was as if he had *known* – yet how could anyone have known, Talgarth least of all, that a bolt from the blue would end things for her and Tarquin, and she would run away to Cornwall to try and forget!

'It's an interesting place,' said Hugh, and then he held her by the shoulders and smiled down at her, a trifle sadly. 'I shall miss you, Ruan. Will you write to me?'

'Yes. You'll want to know how Yseult is faring.'

'I shall want to hear how things are with you, as well.' His eyes were serious. 'You must have guessed that I find you a rare sort of girl, with a very kind heart.'

'Thank you, Hugh.'

'Don't be polite!' He gave her a slight shake. 'I'm not so set in my ways that I can't feel the urge to kiss a girl, and you ask for it when you act all innocent, as if you're with your favourite uncle.'

'I don't want to lose your friendship,' she said gravely.

'You think a kiss would spoil it?'

'It might, Hugh. We're not surface people who can play at love as if it were a game, and you know how I feel about Tarquin. It wasn't just a case of girl meets handsome actor and becomes infatuated. It went deeper than that ... these coming weeks in Cornwall will prove how deep.'

He looked into her wide eyes and nodded. 'Born wise, aren't you, Ruan, for all your youth? Yes, you must face the proving time. You must find out by yourself how much of your heart is irretrievably lost to Tarquin Powers.'

A few minutes later they said goodbye and Ruan went to her hotel room to pack the clothes she had bought for the coming weeks at Pencarne. A couple of pretty dresses, one of them the colour of a watermelon. Cotton shirts and crisp blue jeans for the beach. A bathing suit of sunny gold, and a short, swinging green skirt for moorland walking, with green casuals to match. She had already a suede stormcoat with a lambswool collar in case of tricky weather, the moorland mists Hugh had mentioned.

Quite soon her suitcase was packed and ready, and there was nothing more to do except wait. She had no letters to write, no more telephone calls to make. She had phoned Ann Destry earlier that day and been told that Tarquin was making good progress. She had wanted to say: 'Give him my love,' but the words would have no meaning from the stranger she had become to him.

Ann knew she was off to Cornwall and had wished her luck. 'They say, my dear, that when you cross the Tamar you're in another world. Perhaps you will find Cornwall more your world than ours might have been.'

Ruan wandered to the window of her hotel room and saw that the roofs of the passing buses were wet with rain. It seemed as if it had been raining each time something momentous had happened to her.

In many ways doth the full heart reveal
The presence of the love it would conceal.

E. COLERIDGE

Part Two

CHAPTER SIX

FALCON'S TOR, a hooded frown of a rock dark against the sky over the wide expanse of the moors above Pencarne, a charming fishing village tucked beneath the craggy wing of the cliffs.

The cottage itself was as if enchanted, tucked away on its own ledge of rock, with a garden spilling down a rocky terrace. The rooms were furnished in a comfortable country style, and the kitchen was equipped with a gas cooker, food cupboards, a heater for the bath, and a small gas fridge.

Jem Lovibond had been as nice as his name and had carried all her groceries from the village stores, and being the only son of his mother had even helped to spread bed linen over the lavender bushes to dry in the wind off the sea. 'You'm a little lass yourself to have the care of doctor's young un,' he said to her, his smile broad and friendly. 'Miss Yseult be coming tomorrer and a bit of a tease she be, for all her frail looks. Now if there's anything else I can be doing for you, Miss Perry, you just let me know.'

'Thank you, Jem.' She smiled back at him. 'Is everyone hereabouts as kind as yourself?'

'We're neighbourly,' he said with gruff shyness. 'You'm not all that foreign, not with your looks and that first name of your'n. 'Tis Cornish as I am!'

He ambled away in tall seaboots, as rugged as the rocks themselves, with a big, kind, simple heart. Ruan took deep breaths of the Cornish air and felt certain she would like this place. Even from here she could hear the sea, and knew that at night it lapped in its rhythm those who slept in the cottages of Pencarne.

The next hour or so passed busily, for she gave the cottage a thorough airing, made a batch of cakes and butter scones, and put flowers in all the rooms. By the time she was finished everything looked bright and welcoming, and smelled of cakes fresh from the oven.

She gazed around her with satisfaction, decided she had earned a cup of tea and one of her own cakes, and sat down to enjoy them in the sunlit kitchen.

She glanced at the clock and saw that it was five-thirty. In a while Ann and Buckley would be going to the hospital to visit Tarquin. They would talk of the theatre, and of his convalescence. They would discuss Ann's wedding, but there would be no mention of the part Ruan had played in the dramatic events of the past few weeks.

Everything blurred and she battled with her quick, lonely tears. She mustn't sit here thinking . . . she would go for a walk! She jumped to her feet, ran a comb through her hair, grabbed her suede jacket and walked out into the reddening sunlight of evening. A wind had risen from the beach below and it blew cool against her eyes, and revived her with its freshness.

She took the winding path that led down past the Lovibond cottage, its front garden a mass of flowers, growing and clinging together in the rocks and crannies, with fantastic seashells set here and there. Jem's mother was in the garden, cutting some mint from a window box. 'Takin' a walk to the beach?' she called out.

'Yes, it's such a fine evening.' Ruan stood on the path, her hair blowing in the wind. 'I do like your garden, Mrs. Lovibond. It's a picture.'

'You're kind to say so.' The woman shaded her eyes from the blaze of the westering sun. 'The tide will soon be turning, so you mind yourself, girl.'

'I can swim,' Ruan laughed.

'Aye, but are you used to our Cornish swells? They'd toss a dinky piece the likes of you like a cork on the water. You mind, now.'

'Of course,' Ruan said at once, and it was nice of people to be concerned over her. She waved and continued on her way down the cliff path to the shore, smiling to be called 'a dinky piece', and catching her breath at the long sweep of the sands, where the rocks were like sleeping sea-monsters, their snouts in the creaming water. She gazed for a long time, both thrilled and awed by this legendary sea-coast, with the high-flying spray that spoke of a temper to these waters that could be dangerous. Seagulls swooped near, mewing as they flew by, to land on the rocks with perfect grace. They alone shared the beach with Ruan, and she could well imagine how wild and desolate this coast had been in the bad old days when ships had been lured to the rocks by the lanterns of the Cornish wreckers, when the caves had been used for hiding kegs of smuggled brandy, and parcels of fine lace.

Bearing in mind that soon the tide would turn, she went only as far as some stranded rocks, warn smooth by the sea and the wind, and providing a perch so she could watch the spume and tumult of the rising tide, the cliffs rising in craggy tiers behind her, made tawny by the setting sun. It was bold and stirring scenery, and Ruan was held by it as if entranced. It was Byronic, with the sun dipping into the sea and being slowly extinguished in the water.

Everything was quiet, except for the seabirds calling and the waves splashing ever higher over the sea-held rocks. Ruan thought herself entirely alone, and then distinctly she heard a galloping sound along the beach, coming nearer every second, until a dark horse and its rider were outlined against the sunset and the racing waves. She sat very still on her rock, until some instinct, some forewarning, drove her to her feet . . . just as the horse came splashing close by, sending up spray and sand from its hooves.

Her sudden movement must have startled the animal, for he gave a sudden whinny and reared up on his hind legs, almost throwing his rider out of the saddle.

'Who the devil's that?' As quick as he was strong the rider hauled on the bridle and controlled the horse, then he glanced round to see the cause of the trouble. His black hair blew in the wind, and the tossing mane of the horse was just as dark and wild. There was something primeval about the pair, as if they had appeared from one of the great caves, to take sole possession of the beach when the sun went down and the waves rode in from the sea.

Ruan stared at the man, the last of the light caught in the deep blue of his eyes. She would have known him anywhere . . . here on this remote Cornish beach, with the waves beating at the rocks, he was in his element, unmistakable, a part of the timeless scene.

'So we meet again,' he said, raising his deep voice above the rising tempo of the tide. 'You came, after all, to see my part of the world. What brought you, Ruan Perry? Not any liking for me, I'm sure.'

He smiled as he spoke and cantered his horse towards her, reining in beside her slim, taut figure. He gazed down at her, a look of challenge in his eyes. 'Will you shake hands with me, so I'll know you're not some imp made out of seaweed and spells, put here to startle my horse so he'd maybe throw me to the rocks?'

'You always said strange things, Mr. Talgarth.' She tossed her hair, which was growing damp from the spray in the air. 'I must go back, and you had better ride on, if you don't want to get caught by the tide.'

'Where are you staying?' he demanded.

She didn't want to tell him, but knew he was obstinate enough to keep her here until the water was around her ankles. 'I'm staying here in Pencarne, as holiday companion to the young daughter of a – a friend of mine.'

He gestured towards the cliffs with his whip. 'At one of the cottages?'

'Yes,' she spoke reluctantly. 'Rock Haven Cottage.'

'Ah, that's interesting. And now you'd better run home to your haven before I have to snatch you away on the back of Sable!'

She gave him a wide-eyed look, then ran in the direction of the cliff steps. His laughter followed her, mingling with the sound of the sea as it washed over the shingle to the sand. Halfway up the steps Ruan felt compelled to turn and gaze after the rider and his horse until they were swallowed up far along the sands. So it was in that direction that St. Avrell lay, and there would be no escape from further meetings with Eduard Talgarth.

Her heart beat fast, for what was it Charme had said? 'He wants someone to share his chateau – he might have proposed to you, if you hadn't shown so plainly that you thought him hateful.'

Suddenly she felt afraid. What if there was some truth in her stepsister's remark? What if he meant to pursue her, now he found her again in this remote part of the country? He had been a trader in deep waters, where men thought nothing of pirating pearls. He looked as if it would amuse him to pursue a girl against her will.

She ran on up the steps, as if already she heard his tread behind her. It was crazy to behave in this way, yet she didn't stop running until she reached the cottage and let herself in. She switched on the light and stood with her back against the closed door. She breathed unevenly, and her spray-damp hair clung in russet tendrils to her wind-flushed cheeks. In a while, her breath regained, she gave a scornful little laugh. As if Eduard Talgarth could gain some hold over her if she didn't wish it! This was not the mysterious East, or Victorian England. In this day and age a girl had no need to fear any man!

She was about to go through to the sitting-room when she noticed a covered dish on the kitchen table. She paused to lift the cover and a delicious aroma of cold pickled pilchards whetted her appetite. There was also an apple pasty and a little jug of cream, and a sunflower plucked from the Lovibond garden to let her know who had called and left her a Cornish supper.

'They're dears,' she whispered, and she sat down to enjoy the food, pushing to the back of her mind a dark face lit by a pair of dangerous blue eyes.

Strange that blue eyes could give that impression, as if a flame burned in them!

She went to bed about nine and read for a while by the light of a fat little brass lamp. Her room was charming, with a door connecting it to the bedroom in which Yseult had books and belongings left over from last year's holiday – boxes of shells and curl-edged photographs pinned to a cupboard door, sea-faded shorts, and an old brass bell picked up from the shore, washed there from a boat that had met disaster, perhaps, on a stormy night.

Ruan could hear the sea as she lay alone in the cottage, but she wasn't nervous. Tonight the sea was calm, lapping the shore in a constant rhythm that was like a long-drawn whisper. 'Sleep and dream. Sleep and dream.'

She put out the lamp and settled down drowsily. Tomorrow she would meet her young charge – a rather ancient taxi from the village was picking her up in the morning – and it would cross the moors and take the road to Port Perryn, where the steamer from Brittany would land her passengers. Ruan was eager to meet Yseult, curious to find out if she had her father's kind nature. Hugh Strathern was very kind once a girl grew used to his bluntness, and it gave Ruan a feeling of security to know she could turn to him if anything really frightened her, or worried her.

She closed her eyes in the darkness and listened to the sea ... and though she didn't want to remember that strange encounter on the beach, she found that each detail of it had imposed itself on her mind. She even seemed to smell again the salt tang of the turning tide and the glossy hide of a healthy, well-exercised horse. She saw the iron-dark head of the rider outlined against the fiery glow of the sunset; the strong, sun-weathered face was one she would like to forget ... if she could.

His mouth was etched by deep lines, those of authority, and a rather bold laughter. He had never been a man to dream away the hours; he had been active all his life, and he had been amused by much that he had seen. His nose was dominant, his chin deeply clefted ... as if a devil lurked there. His voice held foreign intonations, a heritage of the Breton in him, intensified by years of travel in far-away places. He ran deep, did Eduard Talgarth, like one of those lonely pools on the moors. Like the sea at his door, and in his blood.

He was born ruthless, or taught by life to be so, and she was resolved to keep out of his way as much as possible. She wasn't going to be pursued like a doe glimpsed in a thicket, who might accord him the amusement of a chase. She had no time for someone who thought of women in that way ... she had known the joy of being loved, and as far as she could see there was no tenderness of heart in the man who was so unlike Tarquin.

Tarquin ... she murmured his name as she drifted off to sleep.

Ruan shaded her eyes from the sunlit water of the bay as the steamer tied up at the jetty. In a short time her passengers began to come ashore, where passports and papers were checked by men in dark blue uniforms. Luggage began to appear in stacks on the quay, where cars and taxis stood at the ready.

There on the quay Ruan watched eagerly for a red-haired schoolgirl accompanied by a nun in a starched white wimple and grey gown. Minutes passed as more and more passengers flocked off the steamer, until as the crowd thinned Ruan caught sight of the tall, thin figure of a grey-clad nun. She half-raised her hand, catching sight of Yseult in the same instant that the girl caught sight of her. She was wearing a Panama hat, but Ruan felt sure she must be Yseult. The girl stared at her, wonderingly, then turned and spoke quickly to Sister Grace. They both looked again in Ruan's direction. The girl was now smiling, but there was a frown on the nun's face as she scanned Ruan from head to foot.

Ruan's dress was the colour of a watermelon, the light, short skirt fluttering in the breeze off the sea. Her russet hair was brushed smoothly back to reveal her slender neck. She was slim, standing there, as insubstantial as if she had drifted out of the heather standing high on the cliffs above the harbour.

As soon as Sister Grace came ashore, and the two passports were checked, she came bearing down on Ruan, a well strapped leather hat-box in one hand, and her charge firmly held in the other one. Her crisp white wimple seemed to add to her height and her dignity, and to reduce Ruan to almost another schoolgirl.

'You are Miss Perry?' she demanded. 'Who is to be chaperone to the young Yseult?'

'Yes, Sister.' Ruan was on the defensive at once. 'I assure you her father, Mr. Strathern, has complete confidence in me.'

'You're very young, not much older than Yseult herself. How will you cope? The two of you alone in a cottage on the moors?'

'The cottage is not on the moors, Sister.' Ruan smiled, but it was not returned. 'Quite close by is the cottage of a fisherman and his mother, two kind people who work for Mr. Strathern.'

'This woman does the cooking?'

'Why, no, I can cook myself.' Ruan was beginning to feel harassed. 'I'm perfectly capable, Sister. Yseult's father would not have given me the job of looking after her if I were irresponsible.'

'Men are not always good judges of the female character,' said Sister Grace explicitly. 'They are too often carried away by a charming face.'

'I'm hardly a vamp—' Ruan didn't know whether to feel amused or annoyed. Yseult was looking at her with sparkling green eyes; she thought this a game, but Ruan knew that the earnest Breton teacher was very reluctant to hand over her pupil to someone so youthful. She could have realized, and dressed her person and her hair with more sedateness. But she had thought only to please Yseult, who had written so eagerly to Hugh about the summer holidays.

'You will forgive me if I am concerned.' Sister Grace shot a fond glance at her pupil. 'Yseult has not been very well, and we at the convent school worry about her. I realize that Monsieur Strathern must be a busy man, but all the same—'

'Mr. Strathern must have written to the school, Sister, to let you know that someone a little younger would be taking care of his daughter? You must allow that a man in his position would be unlikely to choose a companion for Yseult whom he could not trust.' Ruan's smile became coaxing. 'I'm a working girl, Sister Grace, and quite soon I shall be twenty. You mustn't hold my look of youth against me.'

'You feel I am being officious?' For the first time Sister Grace smiled. 'Perhaps I take my duties too seriously and expect it of every person I meet. As you say, Monsieur Strathern is an important man and perhaps more used to judging character than other men. Perhaps you are a nurse, Miss Perry?'

'No, my work is concerned with antiques.'

'Though you look so young.' Sister Grace laughed at her own joke and then became serious again. She turned to Yseult and fussed with her Panama hat. 'You will be a good child, eh? You will keep your hat on in the sunshine and not overtire yourself in the turbulent waters of this Cornwall you are so in love with. Now you will promise me—?'

'Dear Sister Grace, don't be stuffy!' Yseult smiled and her rather pale face took on a puckish charm. 'Ruan looks terribly nice to me, and fun, and I just love that father of mine for giving her to me for the holidays.'

'Then it is settled – child, where is your suitcase?'

'Back there among that lot.' Yseult pointed along the quay, to where the luggage had been piled up.

'Then fetch it this instance! You have all your things in it, with the lace.'

'Lace!' Yseult pulled a face as she went off to find her suitcase.

'A dear child, but a trifle obstinate,' said Sister Grace. 'You will be firm with her, Miss Perry? It isn't good for the young to have all their own way, especially these days, when parents seem to be losing all their authority. Yseult is not one of the strongest, you understand, and she so likes to go into the water. You must watch her. She is subject to bad chest colds.'

'I promised her father that I'd take the very best care of her. He loves her so much, and wants her to have a lovely holiday.' Ruan watched as Yseult returned carrying her suitcase. She had long coltish legs, and it was probably the school uniform that made her look younger than her sixteen years. Her eyes were her father's, and a red-gold plait was escaping from under that ridiculous hat. Ruan decided to buy her a raffish sunhat as soon as Sister Grace departed. The good Sister meant well, but she seemed to lack a sense of fun and humour, to which the young responded with all their instincts.

The three of them made their way off the quayside, and the Sister asked if they were returning right away to the cottage at Pencarne.

'No, I thought we'd have lunch at some quaint place, and have a look round Port Perryn before going home.' Ruan smiled as she spoke, but her tone was firm. She would take good care of Yseult, but she wasn't going to cosset her in cotton wool. Hugh had ordered plenty of fresh air and Cornish cream, and Ruan was going to see that her charge enjoyed plenty of both.

'Will you join us for lunch, Sister?' she asked politely.

Sister Grace replied with regret that she couldn't. She was anxious to get to her sister's bedside. She looked around for a taxi, and it was a relief when the vehicle rolled away with the good woman inside, still holding on firmly to the leather hatbox that contained her clothing, her books and no doubt a few Breton jams and pies for her sister, who was recovering from an operation.

'She's a good soul, but—' Yseult shot an old-fashioned smile at Ruan – 'why are very good people so very earnest?'

'They see only their duty and are a little afraid of having fun, but without them our world would be terribly wicked.' Ruan took Yseult's suitcase and carried it. 'We'll go and eat at a place I noticed called the Camelot.'

'I rather like wicked people,' Yseult grinned, and removed her hat. Her hair was colourful as old Irish gold, and at once her face took on a piquancy the Panama hat had concealed. 'Nice-wicked, if you know what I mean? Bold but not sold to the devil. There are people like that. Sir Lancelot was one of them . . . all this part of the country is teeming with legends about King Arthur and his Knights!'

'I take it Sir Lancelot is your favourite?' Ruan smiled.

'You bet! He was so brave and daring, and it's sad that he couldn't enter the Company of the Grail because he loved the queen. He's more human than Galahad, who's a bit of a prig.' Yseult's green eyes were gemlike as they met Ruan's, and she swung her school hat by its ribbon as they walked along. 'How did you meet my father? It was a thrill when he wrote to say that he'd found someone young and rather lovely to be my summer companion. You are rather lovely, aren't you? Is Pops taken with you? That would be something! Men get set in their ways without a woman around to keep the atmosphere alive.'

'Really!' Ruan couldn't help laughing. 'Your father operated on a – a friend of mine and saved his life. That's how we met. I needed a job and he suggested that I chaperone you for the summer.'

'Maybe he thought we could chaperone each other,' Yseult suggested, a gleam of devilment in her eyes. 'Pops is awfully nice, isn't he? The rugged sort. I like men who look as if they could take charge of the world – men with authority. I mean to marry one, that is if I can find one who won't mind that I have red hair.'

'It's red-gold, Yseult, and very unusual.'

'The girls at school say I'm ginger. They call me Gingerbush.'

'I shouldn't mind that, Yseult. The ginger-bush smells heavenly, and your man of authority will want a girl with spirit.'

'You're nice, Ruan. You talk to me as if I were grown up.'

'You're on the way, aren't you?'

'Um, but sixteen is such an awkward sort of age, the end

of being a tame schoolgirl who can't do her sums right, and the beginning of being curious about everything. I used to read the tales of the Round Table as if they were fables, now I realize that they're love stories.'

'Doesn't it make life more exciting?' Ruan smiled.

Yseult nodded, and then gave a chuckle of delight. 'This is going to be a super holiday. Cousin Val used to make me feel a complete kid. I couldn't paddle without my rubber shoes on, and she had a fit if I went off with Jem in the boat.'

'We'll do our best to make it a holiday to remember,' Ruan promised. 'This is my first visit to Cornwall and I'm very impressed by the great cliffs and the wonderful stretches of beach. It's almost a world apart.'

' "Into Bodmin and out of the world," ' quoted Yseult. 'The Cornish people are a race apart, and some of them look as dark and foreign as Latin men. It's an exciting place, Ruan. Anything could happen.'

'I'm sure of it.' Ruan looked about her with pleasure in Port Perryn, with its maze of cobbled streets, stout little houses of moorland stone, and long harbour wall draped with fishing nets. The music of the place was the mewing of the gulls, and the singing of a fisherman as he caulked his boat. The air was tangy from the wide Atlantic that surged beyond the tideline, a lion of a sea dabbing at the shingle with paws of velvet this morning.

It delighted Yseult to be lunching at the Camelot, with the figure of a mounted knight above the mullioned windows. And she couldn't get over it when Ruan said she could have a shandy while they waited for their lunch. 'You are a sport – um, I think I'll have lobster, though shellfish is inclined to make me feel itchy.'

'Have the celery soup, and then the lamb cutlets with sprouts and potatoes,' Ruan suggested.

'Are you having that?'

'Yes, it sounds nice, and you don't want to feel itchy all the afternoon.'

'No – all right, I'll have the same as you.'

Ruan ordered their meal and felt pleased. The girl was very thin, and she had promised Hugh a more robust daughter by the end of the summer.

It was over lunch that Yseult asked the inevitable question. 'Where do you come from? Did you meet my father in London?'

Ruan shook her head, and then taking a deep breath she talked of Avendon and tried not to think of the man who had made it a heavenly place, until he had looked at her with a stranger's eyes and she had fled from every reminder of him. The river and the swans, the lightning-struck theatre, and the bridge by the watermill. Only this far away from him could she talk of those places.

'Are you fond of the theatre?' asked Yseult, innocently unaware of the stab to Ruan's heart.

'Yes, I've always enjoyed playgoing. Now what shall we have for dessert? You choose, Yseult.'

'Mmm, we'll have something I bet you've never tasted before – thunder and lightning!'

Ruan stared at Yseult and for a moment her eyes were filled with the pain and shock of seeing the Mask Theatre after it had been struck from the skies.

'It isn't that bad,' laughed Yseult. 'Cornish splits with treacle and cream are heavenly – the people hereabouts call them thunder and lightning.'

'Oh, I see.' Ruan forced a smile to her lips, though a shadow lingered in her eyes. 'Yes, I must try everything Cornish.'

The splits were delectable, and in a while Yseult's chatter eased the awakened throb of pain and loss. By the time they left the inn and wandered down a cobbled lane to where tiny, quaint shops were situated, Ruan was feeling less acutely her longing to see Tarquin; to hear him speak her name, to feel him holding her hand.

They came to a shop with beach things displayed, sand shoes and raffia hats among them. 'You must have a sun-hat,' Ruan said. 'How about the raffish one with the green band to match your eyes?'

'I'm game, if you'll have one as well, Ruan.'

They emerged laughing from the shop, each clad in a high-crowned straw hat. They were bound for the seashore, having left Yseult's suitcase at the inn to be collected when it was time to go home to the cottage. 'I'm glad Sister Grace can't see me, minus my Panama and my blue blazer.' Yseult caught at Ruan's hand and they went running down the slope to the seashore. A man seated on the keel of an upturned boat turned a lazy dark head to watch them, the smoke of a cheroot drifting past the glint of his blue eyes.

As the two girls reached the sand, Yseult suddenly stood stock still and stared at the man on the boat. 'That's a friend of Pops',' she exclaimed. 'I wonder what he's doing in Port Perryn?'

Ruan wondered as well as she recognized that still, strong figure, like a figurehead outlined by the sea and the sunlight.

'He used to sail all over the seven seas,' Yseult whispered excitedly. 'But now he's given it up to settle down with his first love.'

'She must love him to have waited while he sailed all over the place,' said Ruan, slightly puzzled when she remembered the things Charme had said about him.

'I'm not taking about a girl,' Yseult laughed, a young and musical sound that must have carried to the man who sat alone, smoking. 'If he had ever loved a Cornish girl he would have taken her to sea with him – he's that sort, Ruan.'

'Then what are you talking about?' Ruan was intrigued against her will.

'He was to have been a sculptor, and then his father died bankrupt – he was such a gambler that he was a legend in Cornwall – and Eduard Talgarth had to go away to sea to restore the family fortunes. He succeeded! And he bought back the family home, and even some of the scattered treasures, such as old portraits and furniture made from the timber of Armada ships. He's a terribly determined man, and exciting in a way.'

'Exciting?' Ruan murmured, and she was looking at him

as he rose to his feet and began to approach Yseult and herself, his strides long and deliberate across the shingle. He wore well-tailored modern slacks and a white sports shirt, but still he gave the impression of another century, another time, with the smouldering quality of the Cornish added to it. The wind stirred his hair and his shirt sleeves, and his eyes glinted in the sunlight.

'They say there's a devil in him,' whispered Yseult. 'There always is, in the Talgarths.'

'It's young Yseult! I met you last year when you came to St. Avrell with your father.' He held out a hand to Yseult, who was blushing madly as she shook hands with him. His smile was a teasing twist of his lip, as if he knew full well that the two girls had been discussing him.

'Hullo, Mr. Talgarth—'

'Didn't we decide that it would be Eduard?'

'Yes, but I thought you might have forgotten.'

'I never forget the people I want to remember.' He turned a deliberate eye on Ruan, who stood there slim and tense in her soft dress blown by the wind, acutely conscious of the gaze of his vivid blue eyes.

'This is my companion,' said Yseult eagerly. 'Ruan Perry.'

'Miss Perry and I have met already. What, didn't she tell you?' He laughed and looked at Ruan with a mocking light in his eyes. 'By a strange twist of fate we meet again, and I'm curious to know why she came to Cornwall of all places.'

'Because my father asked her to,' Yseult was looking from one to the other with inquisitive green eyes. 'Ruan had a friend who was very ill, and Pops did the operation. She was so grateful to him that she agreed to look after his erring daughter for the summer.'

'How generous of you, Miss Perry, and how nice for Yseult to have you to herself for the summer.' His eyes looked right into Ruan's and their blue was like a wicked flame dancing around the dark pupils, amid the black lashes. 'Would this friend of yours be known to me? Someone I might have met during my stay at Avendon?'

'I – I believe you met him at my stepsister's *masque*. I know you saw him when he played in Shakespeare at the Mask Theatre.'

'Ah, the handsome actor!'

'Yes.' Her heart was beating rapidly, and she felt that uprush of antagonism, that longing to hurt this man who seemed to laugh at her, as if she were the most innocent of all the women he had met during his voyages.

'So he fell ill? Dangerously?'

'He was badly hurt when lightning struck the theatre. Mr. Strathern's great skill saved his life.'

'And you came to Cornwall.'

'As you can see, Mr. Talgarth.' Her chin was tilted, and she braved the searching look she was given by this man who had known of her friendship with Tarquin . . . who had said that stardust in her eyes would be bound to hurt. It was disturbing to think that Eduard Talgarth could read her eyes and know that she had run away because Tarquin no longer loved her.

'Ruan, you are a dark horse,' Yseult broke in. 'You never let on that you knew Mr. Talgarth!'

'It was a passing acquaintance,' he drawled. 'Perhaps Miss Perry had no wish to renew it. All the same, it's nice to see you two girls just as I was feeling a mite lonesome.'

'You looked it.' Yseult smiled at him. 'What are you doing here in Port Perryn today of all days, when I arrive home for my holiday? Did Pops write and tell you?'

'No.' His smile was teasing. 'I haven't been in touch with your father.'

'Then you're a sorcerer! They always have blue eyes.'

'And long white beards,' he drawled.

Yseult laughed. 'Everyone says your grandmother had second sight and could foretell the future. She predicted that the chateau would go out of your family for many years.'

'Only because she knew her son and his fondness for the

cards.' He quirked a black eyebrow and shot his blue glance at Ruan. 'Have you told Miss Perry about the Talgarth devil, which can only be exorcized from each male member of the clan by the love of a true-hearted girl?'

'It's an intriguing story,' Ruan murmured, and her eyes dwelt briefly on his clefted chin. 'But do you believe it, Mr. Talgarth?'

'Having travelled widely and seen quite a few strange things, I'm willing to wonder if it might be wise of the last of the Talgarths to get himself a bride.' He smiled in his bold way. 'A loving bride, that is.'

'I'm sure you won't have any trouble finding one,' said Yseult, her eyes on his broad shoulders and his skin as tanned as oak against his spotless white shirt. 'I wish I'd known you when you were nineteen, when you won the wrestling cup for beating the champion of Penzance.'

'Do you, my gilly?' He looked indulgent. 'Let me see, I could have pushed you out in your baby carriage, but don't know what that would have done to my wrestling reputation.'

'Don't be a tease,' Yseult pleaded. 'I should like to have been about sixteen.'

'I was just setting sail for the Far East, gilly. We'd have waved good-bye for a long, long time.'

'Wouldn't you have taken me with you, if I'd been your girl?'

'I wasn't master of my own ship in those days, Yseult.'

'Do you miss the sea? Is that why you come to Port Perryn to look at the boats?'

'Yes, clinging to memories as if tomorrow can never be as good as the days we've already lived through, with their happy hours, and their sad ones.'

Ruan looked at him as he spoke, so tall and dark with the blue horizon behind him and the blue sea in his eyes. So keen-sighted, so aware, making her feel defenceless as he met her look and asked her without words that they please young Yseult by being friends.

'I must get you two to make up.' Yseult turned to Ruan

and there in her green eyes was that look of the young that pleads for love and laughter and no more bitter words. 'Be a good sport, Ruan. We won't get invited to the chateau if you don't shake hands with Eduard and forget whatever silly tiff you've had. The chateau's so strange and marvellous, here in Cornwall.'

'Is it?' Ruan murmured, and on impulse she held out her hand to Eduard Talgarth and braced herself for the touch of those lean fingers that could take stone, silver, or iron, and shape it to his will.

His fingers took hold of hers and it was a tiny shock, the curious gentleness of his touch, as if her hand were a bird. His eyes dwelt on her blue scarab ring. 'That looks like the real thing,' he said. 'Is it inscribed? They sometimes are, in tiny script under the jewelled wings.'

'There are some words,' she admitted, the warmth of his fingers still about hers, 'but I can't make them out.'

'May I try?'

She hesitated, and then catching Yseult's eager look she drew off the ring and handed it to Eduard, who held it to the sun and studied it for several minutes.

'Yes, the script is in Arabic,' he said finally. 'I can't translate the words for you, but the ring is a talisman to guard you against misfortune.'

She looked at him quickly and wondered if he had guessed who had given her the ring. Its possession had not been lucky for her, though she treasured it for the memories it brought.

'May I try it on, Ruan?' Yseult coaxed. 'It's so unusual.'

'No.' Eduard shook his head and reached for Ruan's right hand. He replaced the ring on her middle finger. 'The scarab is like a marriage ring, it might lose its magic if someone else wears it. I have a ring at the chateau which I'll give you, my gilly, when you both come to dine there with me.'

'What sort of ring?' Yseult looked enchanted by the idea of receiving such a gift from him.

'A princess ring, as worn by the lovely Thai dancers

when they perform their ritual dances in the temple court-yards.'

'I shall love it.' Yseult hugged Ruan around the waist, as if too smitten by sudden shyness to hug the man who looked at her with lazily amused eyes ... blue as Ruan's scarab.

'Have you travelled all over the world?' she asked eagerly. 'Even as far as the Himalayas?'

'Yes, I've visited the mystic temples which perch among the hills of Katmandu, where the bells ring as if made of silver ice. I've seen golden domes burning in the sun, have lived in a teahouse on a bamboo bridge, slept on a couch of Sumatran tiger pelts, and enjoyed the friendship of an old prince of Manchuria.' He smiled and his nostrils tensed as he breathed the tangy Cornish air, whipped to the shore by the wind. 'Now I've come home to St. Avrell – the last of the Talgarths.'

'You are lucky to be a man and able to do just what you like,' said Yseult.

'Not entirely what I like.' He smiled quizzically. 'Now what are your plans for the afternoon? A laze in the sun, then a cream tea, and home to Rock Haven?'

'You are a wizard!' laughed Yseult. 'You must have learned on your travels how to read minds.'

'Perhaps.' His eyes met Ruan's. 'Shall I read yours?'

She smiled a little. 'I'll read yours, Mr. Talgarth. You're at a loose end and wouldn't mind spending the afternoon with us. I'm sure Yseult will be delighted.'

'Can't I delight you?' he drawled.

'Being a mind-reader you should know the answer to that,' she said tartly. She turned away from him, biting the smile on her lips. Did he imagine she wanted his company as much as Yseult wanted it?

They lay on the sun-warmed sand, near where the water rippled over the pebbles, and the drowsy deeps of Eduard's voice came in waves to Ruan. She had tilted her straw hat over her eyes and left him to amuse Yseult with his stories, for like all travellers he seemed to have a store of them, and he possessed also a charm for the younger girl that put Ruan on the defensive. Because he had known about Tarquin he made her remember the things she had run away to forget.

CHAPTER SEVEN

HE knew of a tea-garden where they had delicious clotted cream and chunks of fresh fruit, and it was when they sat replete, enjoying a cool breeze through the acacia trees, that Eduard suggested he drive them home to the cottage.

'I have the jingle with me, if you girls would like to drive back across the moors in the old style?' He held Ruan's gaze with his blue one. 'I'm all for the things of yesterday, with their aura of romance.'

'I've seen you driving the most up-to-date sports car,' she rejoined, though her interest had quickened at his mention of a jingle, one of those spanking, pony-drawn carts which had been so popular in days gone by.

'You've been in my car, haven't you, Miss Perry?' And in a flash there was between them the memory of an evening when she had walked beside the river, across which the theatre had been ablaze with lights. There had been stars in her eyes that evening, and this man had seen them ... and he had seen more, being the sorcerer that Yseult called him. Even then he had known that she would come to the moors, where the heather and the bracken grew high enough to hide a girl.

'A man has to live in today's world,' he said, 'but that doesn't stop him from enjoying the slow boat to the Indies, or a ride in a pony-drawn jingle across the tawny moors.'

'It sounds irresistible.' Yseult stirred out of the daydream in which she had fallen. 'We'd love to come with you!'

'Miss Perry?' He quirked an eyebrow. 'You know you'll enjoy it yourself, so why not give in?'

His eyes challenged her as he sat there with the leaves overhead dappling his pirate-brown face, but for once she couldn't fight him. She was disarmed by the prospect of a drive across the moors. 'We must call at the Camelot to pick up Yseult's suitcase,' she said. He nodded, settled the bill and escorted them to the inn. Fifteen minutes later they were joggling along the homeward road to the tinkle of small bells on the pony's harness. He was a young grey, all dancing legs and mane, trotting briskly past the cob-walled cottages and the village stream where long ago witches had been ducked for loving the devil.

Ruan felt the magic that pervaded the Cornish air as they wended their way past hedges of stone and windbent trees. Eduard's long whip sang in the air but never touched the pony. He pointed out the ruins of an old abbey on a hill, with a twisted black juniper outlined against the reddening sky. 'It looks haunted, eh?' He spoke quite seriously. 'It's said of the chateau that we have a ghost, a French ancestor of mine who stands on a turret to gaze out to sea, waiting for a ship that never came. Legend says he was waiting for his French sweetheart, but she was caught up in the rebellion and never heard of again.'

'What happened to him?' asked Yseult. 'Was his heart broken?'

'He married a Cornish girl,' Eduard smiled. 'They had a daughter who grew up to become the bride of a Talgarth. That is how the chateau came to us.'

'It's a fabulous place!' Yseult's eyes were shining. 'Ruan, it looks as if it belonged in a tale of knights, and damsels in distress.'

'You and your knights!' smiled Ruan.

'All young things have a dream of Tristan, or Hamlet.' A blue glance seemed to pin Ruan. 'They outgrow it – usually.'

She knew at once what he implied, that her love for Tarquin was based on a dream of someone gallant and handsome, who was destined to remain a dream. 'You're wrong, he loved me!' She wanted to fling the words in that dark Cornish face. 'It was love as you could never feel it, you with your sea trader's arrogance, who thinks there is nothing that can't be bought if the right bargain is struck!'

He looked at her as if reading her thoughts, and then

with a laugh he stopped the jingle on a high curve of the road. 'Look,' he murmured, and they watched a firetail winging its way across the moors, flying towards a stone monolith that stood dark and sinister there in the gorse and the bracken that curled about it like golden smoke in the dusk light spreading over the moorland.

'They call it the Devil's Harp,' said Eduard. 'Want to go and hear the wind making music?'

They climbed from the jingle and walked through the waist-high gorse to the monolith, and it was true! The wind around the structure, which took the rough shape of a harp, seemed to produce a weird sound of music, as if an invisible hand played over the dark stone.

'Ooh, I shouldn't care to come to this place on my own.' Yseult caught at Eduard's arm. 'I love these moors in the daylight, but when it begins to get dark they seem to change, to become menacing.'

'The fall of night brings out the primeval in all things,' he said. 'A lover's face takes on a different look; a girl's eyes fill with mystery.'

There was a chime of Celtic music in his voice, and as the wind tugged at Ruan's hair, making the roots tingle, she was aware of being deeply disturbed by the moors and by the man. From among the gorse came the cry of a nightjar, and the afterglow was gold with touches of flame. Vivid scents tangled in the wind ... everything was *moorish and wild, and knotty as a root of heath – hewn in a wild workshop.*'

She caught Eduard Talgarth's gaze upon her, and the afterglow seemed to play in his eyes.

'It's dramatic, isn't it?' he said. 'Like a scene set for a play.'

'Must you?' she whispered.

He quirked an eyebrow and glanced at Yseult, who had gone to pet the pony and was out of earshot if they spoke in low voices. 'Tell me something – did Tarquin Powers tell you before or after he made you love him that he had a wife already?'

'How – how did you know he was married?'

'I made it my business to find out.'

'It was never your business!'

'You say that very emphatically.'

'You came to Avendon as a friend of Charme's.'

'Meaning it was not Charme in whom Powers was taking an interest? I suppose if she had been, then my interest would have been valid?'

'I should have thought so. It was she who drew you to Avendon, and few men who came to the villa ever looked at me, with Charme there.'

'Tarquin Powers looked at you.'

'That was different. We met at the theatre, and though I know now that something about me must have reminded him of his wife, there was a certain magic about our meeting.' Her eyes met Eduard's; in the dusk light his face seemed hard. He was all hardness and angles, like the *menhirs* that stood on the moors. How could he understand how the heart could be touched by a certain look in a pair of eyes; a look that opened the heart because it was somehow lonely. Eduard Talgarth was too self-sufficient to ever need someone as Tarquin had needed her ... if only for a while.

'It was a romantic meeting,' she said quietly.

'Meaning I haven't any romance in me, only a soul of commerce?'

'Am I wrong, Mr. Talgarth?'

'Not entirely. I was never a man to believe in a one and only love, the search for the Grail. There isn't much time for dreaming in the life of a man who trades from port to port, and builds up his own line of ships. The life is too tough, too full of bargaining, as you so rightly guessed. But there is one thing I would never do, rough diamond though I am – I would never make a woman love me knowing I couldn't give her my name ... ah, is that why you ran away, Ruan, because he asked you to be his mistress?'

'I – I loved him. It wouldn't have made me ashamed—'

'Is that why you ran away?' Eduard persisted.

'No – he forgot me after the operation. He didn't know me. He had no recollection of the times we had spent together. Mr. Talgarth, this is rather painful – anyway, why should you be interested?'

'Because you're young, and haven't that shell of self-concern that makes some people safe all their lives. You're like Yseult.'

'Well,' she had to smile, 'it's nice to know that Yseult and myself have your protection – a sort of uncle.'

She heard him catch his breath and knew in an instant that she was in danger from this man who was as much like an uncle as tiger is to tabby cat. With a laugh she ran from him through the gorse to where the jingle stood. Yseult had climbed into the back and fallen asleep, and Ruan held the young, thin figure against her as they jogged home in the dark.

Eduard stopped the jingle at the top of the cliffs, near the path that led down to the cottage. He carried the sleeping Yseult, while Ruan went ahead with the suitcase. She unlocked the front door and switched on the light, and as she turned to Eduard he was framed big and dark in the doorway, a lance of black hair across his forehead, Yseult's red-gold hair spread against his broad shoulder. He looked like a corsair, carrying in his arms his right of plunder. His smile teased Ruan, as if he read her opinion of him in her wide violet eyes.

Yseult stirred as he laid her down on the sofa in the living-room. 'You're home, my gilly,' he said to her.

'Oh, is it all over, our lovely day?'

'There will be others, Yseult, I can promise you.'

She smiled up at him. 'When can we come to the chateau?'

'I'll send word by Medevil. D'you remember him? He's my handyman who used to be a sailor until I left the sea and he came to work for me at the chateau.'

'He told me you saved his life, that he lost part of his left leg to a shark and would have lost the other one if you hadn't dived into the sea with a knife between your teeth.'

Eduard laughed, a bold sound in that cottage room with chintz at the windows. 'Medevil would have managed, somehow. He comes from an island where the people are said to have seven lives. Anyway, he was after pearls when that sea tiger attacked him.'

'The guardian of the pearls,' smiled Yseult.

'Yes, he could well have been that.' Eduard returned her smile and straightened to his great height, so that his dark head seemed about to touch the ceiling beams. 'Good-bye for now, Yseult. Medevil will come with a message when I return from a visit to London. I have to see the captain of one of my cargo ships.'

'Will you see Pops while you're in London?'

'I'm sure of it. I owe him lunch at the Square Rigger.'

'Then you can tell him that I like Ruan very much, and that there's nothing at all for him to worry about.'

Eduard glanced at Ruan. 'You two girls will be okay until I return?'

'Mr. Talgarth, we don't need a tiger couchant at our door. We'll manage perfectly. Tell Hugh so.'

'Hugh?'

'Mr. Strathern,' she said demurely, then gave a gasp as he caught her by the wrist and made her walk with him to the front door. She had but a single thought, that he was going to kiss her! If he did ... well, what would she do? Short of yelling for Jem Lovibond, the only male within reach who measured up physically to this man, who had spent years at sea and who lived by his own rules.

'I can feel you shaking,' he accused. 'What the devil are you thinking – that I want to kiss you in the dark?'

'You're a brute!' she gasped. 'You do your best to em-barrass me.'

'You shouldn't show so plainly, young woman, that you don't like me. It acts as a challenge. I keep getting the urge to reverse your opinion of me.' He caught at her chin and tipped up her face so she had to look at him. 'What is it about me you dislike so much – my lack of sweet talk, my craggy face, or the fact that I warned you that Tarquin

Powers could be heartache for an innocent like you?'

'It must be very satisfying to be always right,' she retorted.

'Meaning you dislike me for all three reasons? Well, it can't be helped. I never had honey on my tongue, or a handsome face, and you can't keep a kitten away from the fire when it's been a long winter. D'you think I didn't guess from the moment I walked into the St. Cyr household that you were treated as a charity child. I came a little too late—'

'What do you mean?' The words broke from her.

'You might have liked me better, Ruan Perry, if I could have been the first man to show you a bit of kindness.'

'Does it matter whether I like you or not?'

'We're going to see a lot of each other during the coming weeks, and that's why I brought you out here. Things are easier said in the dark, and I've this to say. I need friends as much as you – having been away a long time from St. Avrell and having become a stranger to the folk I used to know. Come, Ruan! I don't often ask someone to like me – a little.'

She gazed up at him and his face was just discernible in the porch light that was dim and needed a new bulb in the small lantern hung on a chain. The sighing of the sea could be heard, and it mingled with Ruan's sigh. 'People are so complicated,' she said.

'You mean it isn't easy to like me?'

'You – you must give me time.'

'Did Hugh Strathern have to ask for any?'

'Hugh was there when I needed a friend, and he was kind.' She smiled, for how could she take seriously a cry of loneliness from Eduard Talgarth? That imperious mouth, the deep cleft in his chin, the strong brows bridging the sea-blue eyes, these were the features of a man who held as firmly to his destiny as he had ever held a ship on its course.

He was the last of the Talgarths. He had spent fifteen years of his life earning the money to buy back the family home, and now he must find a girl to marry. There must again be Talgarth children at the chateau, and the line must not be broken as it had been in his father's time. Ruan studied him in the dim light and felt apprehensive of his motive in seeking out a girl like herself. A lonely girl, who had found love and lost it. Who had no family except the St. Cyrs.

She tensed . . . a tremor ran all the way down her spine as his hand touched her hair.

'I'll say good night and leave you in peace,' he said. 'It's what you want more than anything else, eh?'

'I'm tired,' she said, shaken. 'It's been a long day.'

'It should be a relief, Ruan, to know I'll be in London for a week.' He laughed and let her go. 'I'll give your regards to Strathern, and maybe I'll bring you a present from my ship, which has just put in from the East with bales of real silk in the hold.'

'I'd find no use for it, Mr. Talgarth, here in Cornwall.'

'Not even for cushion covers?' he drawled. 'I'll be seeing you, Miss Perry. *Au revoir*.'

He walked away into the night and she heard him mounting the cliff path with long strides. She didn't move until there came the jingle of bells on the pony harness and the clip-clop of hooves, fading away along the road to St. Avrell. The sea murmured far down on the beach and the atmosphere was serene again.

Yseult's voice floated out to her. 'I'm making hot chocolate, Ruan. Do come and drink it before it gets cold.'

Ruan smiled to herself, for hot chocolate and the chatter of her young charge were so normal after her conversation with Eduard Talgarth. Beneath the things they had said to each other there ran undercurrents, a sense of being whirled into a danger she must fight against. He asked for her friendship, offered a gift of silk, yet she couldn't feel at ease with him. His very look made her want to run away from him . . . his touch was unbearable because it wasn't Tarquin's.

Suddenly she closed the cottage door against the darkness and hastened to join Yseult in the living-room.

'What were you two talking about all that time?' she asked. 'And why didn't you tell me you'd met Eduard already? Why so secretive?'

'I didn't think it was important.' Ruan sipped her chocolate. 'We'll go swimming tomorrow, shall we, and have a picnic on the beach?'

'Mmm, super!' Yseult's eyes were a dreamy green over the rim of her cup. 'Do you think Eduard would wait three years for me to grow up? I do think he's lonely, and I'd love to be the mistress of a chateau. It would be the most romantic thing, to be the bride of the last of the Talgarths.'

'I shouldn't think your father would approve of his fledgling in the keeping of a man double her age,' Ruan said dryly.

'But age isn't important when two people care for each other. Elder men are kinder, and more worldly, and they can teach a girl all about life.' Yseult licked chocolate from her lip. 'I bet if I tried I could make Eduard wait for me.'

'You'll do nothing of the sort!' Ruan looked shocked. 'I can't allow you to flirt with Eduard Talgarth. Your father would never forgive me.'

'Are you attracted to Pops?'

'I like him very much.'

'Liking someone isn't the same as being attracted.'

'I don't know where you get all this nonsense from, but it's got to stop.' Ruan spoke firmly. 'Everything is shipshape in your room, and it's time you were in bed.'

'Spoilsport,' said Yseult, and then she looked contrite. 'Does it hurt to talk about romantic things because you can't forget that man you were in love with?'

'I – I won't discuss the subject, Yseult! It's over – I've got to forget about him.'

'Was he terribly handsome?'

'Yes.' Ruan drew Yseult to her feet. 'And now off up the wooden hill to the land of nod, young lady. I'll wash the cups and be up myself in a jiffy.'

'Ruan—'

'What now, Miss Curious?'

'I'm glad Pops asked you to spend the summer with me. It's an awful bind to be treated like a kid, but you and Eduard treat me as if I'm almost grown up. Don't you find him interesting? He's been to so many far places, and there's something about him that makes him exciting. What do you think it is?'

'A dash of the pirate,' said Ruan explicitly. 'He's a man who takes little heed of the rules and conventions other people live by.'

'How did you come to meet him?'

'He came to Avendon to court my stepsister. Charme is very stunning, but too level-headed to be swept off her feet by a bold Cornishman who likes his own way. She chose to become engaged to someone else, but I'm sure Mr. Talgarth's heart wasn't broken, or even a little cracked.'

'You are hard on him,' Yseult protested.

'Oh, I'm sure he can take it,' Ruan smiled. 'It may be salutary for him to meet a female who isn't bowled over by his piratical charm.'

'There, you've admitted he has charm!'

'What man hasn't, when he cares to turn it on? And now to bed, young lady. Your eyes are too big for your face.'

'It's because you're opening them up to drama and mystery, Ruan.' With the sudden affection of the young Yseult put her arms around her youthful chaperone and gave her a warm hug. 'I do like you. You're so different from my teachers, and from Cousin Val. You're like one of those lovelorn damsels who has to be rescued by a knight in armour.'

'From what must I be rescued?' Ruan laughed.

'From being in love with the wrong man.'

Ruan held her breath and then released it. Pain shook her heart. How could the child know that while love had lasted between herself and Tarquin it had been lyrical –

like a song with all the shades and tones just right. But their love had been star-crossed, and something from the sky itself had torn them apart. They had loved one another at the wrong time. They had met too late for their song to last.

Each new day in the week that followed was born with birdsong, the tang of the sea on the air, and its inviting glitter far down the cliffs on which the cottage was perched like the rather precarious nest of a pair of early birds. They would scramble out of bed at the first touch of the sun and be in the water before Mrs. Lovibond had cooked their breakfast.

A wonderful sea of blue dyed with green, with not a cloud in the sky until Saturday morning, when the sea was overcast and the spray was flying high, filling the cove with its clamour. 'Ooh,' Yseult ran out of the waves, 'they grab at you this morning!'

Ruan laughed and munched an apple pasty, sweet with brown sugar. 'Shall we go to Mawgan-in-Vale? We've spent most of the week on the beach and I want to see the tiny smuggling village at the foot of the vale.'

'Yes, let's.' Yseult skipped about on the beach, her hair in a Psyche knot, her face aglow with spray. 'It looks a bit like rain, but we can wear our macs.'

They raced up the cliff path to get ready for their outing. Ruan made ham and tomato sandwiches, filled a flask with coffee, added jam pasties to the pack, and they set off on their hike to Mawgan-in-Vale. The gorse and the bracken shimmered in the wind on the moors, and it took them a couple of hours to reach the village which long ago had been the hideaway of smugglers. Today it looked peaceful enough, with its small colour-washed houses built one below the other, dotting the valley like the dwellings of fairy folk. Narrow crooked streets led downwards, the walls of the houses hung with creepers and fuchsias. Little doors were set aslant in the houses, and cats drowsed on the windowsills among pots of herbs and boxes of pansies, with petals like the wings of moths.

Ruan was enchanted by the place. It was as if time had paused and left it curiously undisturbed. That rugged old Viking smoking a pipe in a doorway might have been a brandy pirate. That girl gaily singing as she hung out washing might have loved a black-haired seaman with bolts of lace hidden beneath the lobster pots in his painted boat.

'I'm glad now,' she thought. 'I'm glad I came to Cornwall.'

The day passed happily. They ate their lunch on a grassy bank, then they explored the village and bought postcards at the little thatched post-office.

'I'm sending a couple to Brittany,' said Yseult. 'And one is for Pops. Who are you sending yours to?'

Ruan studied the coloured cards and thought of Ann Destry – but Ann might no longer be at Avendon. If Tarquin had left the hospital, then Ann and Buckley would have left with him. They had plans for a play in London. Tarquin had a villa just outside Rome . . .

'I've bought them as a keepsake,' she conjured a smile. 'Mawgan-in-Vale is such a pretty place. I shall want to remember our day here.'

It was around four o'clock when the clouds seemed to come a little lower, and the fuchsias on the rambling walls took on deeper shades. A bit of a mizzle was blowing by the time they climbed breathlessly to the moors. A weathered villager passed them, his dark eyes flashing from one young face to the other. 'Hurry you home,' he said. 'Them clouds are going to break over the moors before very long and it's soaked you'll be.'

His words were prophetic, but as luck would have it they had come in sight of the stout white curve of an old mill when the first big drops stung their cheeks.

'Race you!' cried Yseult, and they ran long-legged through the quickening rain, reaching a doorway that yawned darkly in the thick wall as the clouds burst and the rain pelted down. It flattened the heather and washed the granite rocks, and the wind howled weirdly as they stood in the shelter of the mill, deserted and ruinous, but a protection against the downpour.

'We'd have been soaked ... drowned,' gasped Yseult, shaking her wet hair away from her neck. 'It's like being under a waterfall ... hear how it pounds on the roof of this old place!'

Ruan glanced about her and saw steps leading up to another room, where long ago flour was ground between millstones rotated by sails that had long since perished. Something rustled in a far corner and she tried not to think of bats, or the prowl of spiders. It was better here than getting soaked in that deluge ... the moors and the skies seemed blended together by that sheet of rain. It thundered on the roof overhead, and nearby streams could be heard gushing as they filled up and overflowed.

It was awesome, as if the rain meant never to stop, and Ruan tensed herself against a storm such as the one that had hit Avendon. Yseult and herself were alone here, in a derelict mill. What if there was lightning ... she shuddered, and Yseult turned to look at her, with eyes wide and green in the dusky light.

'It's all right,' she soothed. 'Already the rain sounds as if it's easing off.'

And in a while, with a suddenness that brought silence to the moors, the rain ceased. Only the swollen streams gurgled, and the half-drowned gorse and herbage gave off scents that were like a benediction.

Ruan took a deep breath of the wonderful air and smiled at Yseult. 'We'd better make a move while we can,' she said, and they stepped out bravely into the soaking heather and made off across the moors towards Pencarne. The rain had drained out of the sky, leaving it silvery and translucent and the drops of water on the bracken fronds seemed to glitter like gems. It was all rather lovely, but the two girls were wet to the knees by the time they came in sight of the cliffs where the cottage nestled, with its warm stove, a change of dress, and cups of hot sweet tea.

They hastened towards their small haven, and then were

brought up short as they reached the path that led down to the cottage. There was a jagged gap and a wide sluice of mud draining downwards, with clumps of rock and earth mixed in with it. The two girls gasped in unison and stared at the wreck of the cottage, half-buried beneath a great chunk of the cliffside.

'Holy Moses!' Yseult whispered.

Ruan felt the blood leave her face. If Yseult and herself had arrived home before the deluge, then they would have been inside the cottage when the heavy rain had brought down on its roof what a few hours ago had looked like solid rock face.

'What a mess!' Yseult was about to go scrambling down the muddy path when Ruan caught at her arm and held her back. 'No, it's no use going down! Look, someone is there – he's coming up to us!'

They waited as the dark-haired figure climbed towards them, nimble of body and yet curiously awkward.

'It's Medevil!' Yseult exclaimed, and waved her arm excitedly as Eduard Talgarth's servant made his halting way up the dangerously wet and rock-strewn path. As he drew nearer his teak-coloured face was slashed by a wide grin.

'*Mon maître* say I come bring young ladies to tea – looks like young ladies come to stay at chateau all night, maybe longer. That little house a washout, miss.' He looked directly at Ruan. 'Not nice. Got to be cleared of debris from the landslide.'

'What of the people lower down the cliffs?' she asked anxiously. 'Are they all right?'

'Sure.' His white teeth gleamed in a reassuring smile edged by devilry. 'The fall of rock hit the one cottage, miss. I make sure you young ladies not in it, and now I take you to *mon maître*.'

'But our things are in the cottage,' she said. 'Our clothes and personal belongings. We must have those.'

'Mr. Jem, he bring what he can for you, but right now you both a-shivering, and *mon maître* angry with Medevil if I don't bring you straight home to the chateau. Come now! The jingle awaiting for us.'

'Yes, let's go to the chateau.' Yseult caught at Ruan's arm and urged her away from the wreckage. 'Mr. Talgarth will see to everything when he learns what has happened to the cottage. He'll take charge.'

Ruan was in no doubt about that, but there was nothing else to be done and she turned away from the sorry sight of the cottage and walked with Yseult and Medevil to the waiting jingle. Medevil had parked the pony and trap in a sheltered bend of the cliffs, and his dark hand caressed the sprightly animal as the girls climbed into the vehicle and took their seats. Ruan couldn't help looking at the islander who had sailed under Talgarth's command until his encounter with a shark. Now, with his limping agility, he stepped into the jingle, shook the reins, and they went jogging away from Rock Haven in the direction of St. Avrell.

'It's exciting, really.' Now Yseult had recovered from her initial shock, her green eyes were shining. 'We'll be guests at the chateau. Just think of it, Ruan!'

Ruan was doing just that. The one thing she had not bargained for was the enforced company of the master of the chateau, but until the cottage was set to rights she would have to accept the situation. Lodgings could have been found in the village, but Yseult would be disappointed. The chateau was a romantic and unusual place in her young eyes, and Ruan didn't want to add to the distress the girl had felt upon finding the cottage half-buried by the landslide.

The moorland sky was now lemon-tinged, streaked by a deep blue like that on the edge of a flame. The moors looked strange, and the *menhirs* standing here and there had the look of lonely figures entranced by the wand of Merlin.

Ruan felt a small cold hand slide into hers, and she gave Yseult an anxious scrutiny. 'You're going into a hot bath as soon as we reach the chateau,' she said. 'I don't want you catching a cold.'

'I shall be all right . . .' and there Yseult was shaken by
a couple of sneezes.

Medevil turned to look at her. 'You both needs a hot
rum toddy, with a dash of cinnamon, lemon and brown
sugar.' He urged the pony to a faster pace, and the harness bells tinkled, and the wind sang across the heather,
bringing with it the tang of the sea. 'We soon be home,
young misses. We soon reach the chateau.'

CHAPTER EIGHT

THERE it stood against the dusky sky, a tumble of roofs and winding walls and pepperpot turrets lanced by narrow windows, with lanterns alight as they drove into the courtyard.

Chateau of sea mists, and the legend of a French noble who had fled from tyranny to find a restless peace with a Cornish bride.

Ruan's first impulse was to be fascinated, and then she saw a tall figure stride out of a door and her every nerve seemed to steel itself as Eduard Talgarth crossed over to the jingle. 'You've been a devilish time bringing my guests,' he said to Medevil, and then in the lantern light he caught sight of their bedraggled appearance.

'*Mon dieu!*' The Gallic exclamation seemed to come naturally to him, especially within the environs of the chateau. 'You look like a pair of drowned young cats! Did Medevil drive into a moor pool on the way here?'

'There was a landslide right on to the cottage,' Yseult broke in with another sneeze. 'It's in a frightful state and we hope you'll let us stay with you for a while.'

'Were you in the cottage?' His eyes flashed to Ruan and took in her windblown hair around her wide eyes, the tremor of her sensitive mouth.

'We went to Mawgan-in-Vale for the day. We took shelter in an old mill when the rain came down – when we arrived home we found the cottage so damaged that Medevil brought us here. I – I hope you don't mind?'

'Mind?' He looked angry for a moment. 'What do you take me for, Miss Perry, a stone man of the moors? I'm only too glad to have a sound roof to offer you both.'

'Thank you,' she said politely.

'You're welcome.' He glanced at Yseult and broke into a smile. 'You'll be my rights of wreck, eh? Come, out of the jingle and into the chateau with you. There's a great fire, and Medevil will make a couple of his famous rum toddies for you, while Jancey runs your baths. We'll soon have you warm and snug.'

He lifted Yseult to the ground and she ran into the chateau through the door he had left wide open. He extended a hand to Ruan, but she ignored it – and paid the penalty. The cobbles underfoot were still damp from the rain and as she jumped down she slipped and would have fallen if Eduard had not caught hold of her. In an instant she was close to a strength so masculine that she seemed to lose her identity and to become a piece of flotsam he could break and toss aside. She had never experienced anything like it before, and instinct warned her not to struggle or she would touch off the primitive spark in this man.

She heard him laugh very softly. 'You seem adept at landing in the places you would rather avoid. Now ask me to release you.'

'You mean beg, don't you?' As she spoke she felt her heart beating like the wing of a trapped bird.

'Yes, let me hear how you sound when you plead for a little mercy from the stone man.'

'Mr. Talgarth, I'm worried about Yseult and would like to ensure that she gets to bed as soon as possible. She isn't all that strong and had a bad cold just before she came home for the summer.'

'Very well, I'll strike a bargain with you. If you'll call me Eduard I'll let you go.'

'You're being adolescent!'

'No more than you, Ruan. You treat me as if I'm dangerous to know, when all the time I'm an ordinary chap with a fairly kind nature.'

'Ordinary, did you say?'

'For a Cornishman with a dash of the Breton. We are inclined to look like black-browed pirates, but you mustn't let that disturb you.' His teeth glimmered in a taunting smile. 'I'm beginning to be curious about the disturbing effect I seem to have on you, Ruan. Perhaps you secretly like me.'

'I can assure you I don't!'

'Dear, dear, how sure you are, and how quick to deny that I can be likeable. Shall I make you like me?'

'You'd be wasting your time!'

'There's a nervous quiver in your voice, Ruan. And your eyes are wide with apprehension. Have you vowed not to fall in love again just because your wings got singed by a brush with your first flame? It happens to all of us at some time.'

'As it happened to you – with Charme?'

'Your beautiful stepsister.' His arms tightened around Ruan's slimness, as if he remembered a more luscious figure in his embrace. 'She'd have made the perfect mistress for a chateau, don't you agree? The many old rooms would have bloomed under her tasteful touch, and in no time at all the chateau would have been a show place. The balls and weekend parties of my grandmother's time would have been revived, and everyone would have applauded my choice of a bride. Such a shame so romantic a story couldn't come true. Would you have liked me for a brother-in-law, Ruan?'

'As I've left the St. Cyrs, I don't suppose it would have mattered to me.'

His arms were hard around her, no hint of release in them. 'So you're not going back to them?'

'Never.'

'Where will you go when the summer ends?'

'To London – like Dick Whittington.'

He gazed down at her, the glimmer of the lanterns in his eyes, and etching the strong angles of his dark face. 'Hugh Strathern lives there.'

'Yes, Mr. Talgarth.'

'In which case I'd better let you go to his child before you succumb to anxiety neurosis in my arms. There's one more thing.'

'I knew there would have to be.'

A smile flickered at the edge of his mouth. 'Please feel at

home in my chateau. I'm sure you have the imagination to appreciate its romantic history and its grace, built high on Cornish granite. Feel free to explore, and don't let this mishap to the cottage spoil your fun.'

As he spoke he freed her from his arms, and she walked with him into his home. It was like stepping into another century. There was a worn grandeur about the hall, lit by lamps and a great fire that reflected on the tawny panelling that rose to a quaint gallery above the winding staircase. The floor was covered by a massive carpet of mellowed colours. Large canvases hung upon the walls, the furniture had a French look, and there was a sideboard with a wine-holder and glasses. The chimneypiece rose to the ceiling and was carved with figures and masks, and there in a deep armchair Yseult was curled, her feet to the warmth of the flames.

She smiled contentedly at their host. 'I feel like a rescued damsel in the castle of Lancelot,' she said.

He smiled down into her drowsy green eyes. 'I've been telling Ruan that you're welcome to stay at the chateau for as long as you both wish. The house, the gardens, and the beach below are yours to enjoy – though you're not to venture into the water when the seas are riding high. The rocks of St. Avrell are below the surface and rather dangerous.'

He glanced at Ruan, and then drew to the fire a little blue velvet prayer-stool. 'Please sit down. Medevil will fix your hot toddies while I have a few words with Jancey, my housekeeper. You'll find her a bit gruff, but she means well.'

He strode from the hall, and Ruan sat down on the stool near the welcome glow of the fire, its flames blue-edged as if driftwood burned among the coals. On such a night, with the sea breezes joining forces with the moorland wind it was good to be within thick, safe walls. The fire crackled cosily, and the ocean could be heard swirling over those hidden rocks down on the shore.

'Isn't this a fascinating place?' Yseult whispered, as if

144

the portraits listened. 'Do you like that silver goblet on the mantel? That's Eduard's wrestling cup. And look at that model of a sailing ship – he carved every piece with his own hands, and the sails are of silk. I never dreamed when I came here with Pops last year that I would ever live here.'

'Only until the cottage is made habitable,' Ruan warned.

'That could take a week or more.' Yseult wriggled her toes in the firelight. 'He called you Ruan. He made your name sound as it should – why don't you like him, when he's so kind to us? Are you pretending not to like him? Grown-ups sometimes act that way.'

'There are some people we have to get used to, others we can know in an hour.' Ruan leaned to the fire and her russet hair fell forward around her slender face and her reflective violet eyes. 'At Avendon he seemed worldly and cynical like my stepsister's friends. Here at St. Avrell he's different, and I can't make up my mind which is the real Eduard Talgarth.'

'Well,' said Yseult, looking wise, 'I should think he'd be more himself in Cornwall than elsewhere.'

'A man who has travelled all over the globe?' Ruan's gaze dwelt on the carved ship with the silken sails, and she visualized him at the helm of a ship in the sunshot waters of the Indies, firing orders at his crew, the wind in his hair that was so black it had the gleam of a raven's wing, his eyes reflecting the vivid blue of the sea. He was elemental, and therein lay his fascination and his danger, for how could you grasp a wave, or a flash of lightning, or the wing of an eagle?

Ruan couldn't visualize a moment when she would feel at ease with him. The elusive essence of her nature had met a dominance it retreated from – as the willow shields itself from the wind in a cloak of leaves.

It came as a relief when Medevil entered the room carrying a pair of steaming tankards on a tray. The air was at once redolent of the mixed aromas of rum, spice, and lemons. 'These take away the chills,' he grinned. 'Now don't you wrinkle your nose at good rum, Miss Yseult. You pretend it a magic potion and drink every drop.'

Ruan smiled as she sipped the potent toddy. 'You must miss your sunny island, Medevil, where the sugar cane and the spice trees grow?'

He reflected on that, the firelight in his black eyes, agleam with his memories of places and experiences all bound up with the man he had served for many years. 'Maybe no sugar cane grow on the moors,' he said, 'but the sea beat like drums under Medevil's window, and he happy to be here for next five lives.'

'Five, Medevil?' She looked intrigued.

'Lose two others, miss. One in a waterfront fight, when *mon maître* pick me up like sack of taters and carry me aboard with a knife in my ribs. He pull it out, clean the hole with whisky and make Medevil yell so much he come back to life.' The islander grinned, showing his fine white teeth. 'Next time a sea-tiger take me for his lunch, and the cap'n fight off that hungry shark and lug Medevil aboard ship again. Medevil reckon he gotta stay with this man. No safe, without. No smile on sugar island away from *mon maître*.'

An earthy loyalty rang in the words, and Ruan was moved despite her own desire to run away from the man to whom everyone else was so attached.

He returned at that moment with Jancey, who took them upstairs to a pair of adjoining rooms. Soon they had bathed, and were given flannelette nightgowns to wear in bed. Yseult decided that her four-poster was too big, and she was nervous of the cavernous cupboards in case they harboured mice.

'Let me sleep with you, Ruan?' she pleaded.

'Jump in then.' Ruan had to smile at the comical picture they made in her own huge bed – Persian, with inlay, to match the furniture with dragons carved all over it. Surely such a bed had never been slept in before by a couple of waifs, their hair plaited above the ribbon-drawn necks of flannelette nighties!

Yseult gave a giggle, and then the door swept open and Jancey marched in with a large tray on which there was a cluster of covered dishes. 'Don't you like your room?' She gave Yseult a stern look.

'It's rather big – and I couldn't help thinking of the chateau ghost.'

'Ghosts won't hurt you, my girl, they're made out of superstition and shadows.' Jancey settled the tray between the two girls. 'It's people cause the trouble and strife.'

'I'm sorry our arrival has caused you more work,' Ruan apologized. 'I'll keep our rooms tidy, and help with the meals if you'd like me to.'

'There's no need for you to clutter my kitchen.' Jancey swept a gimlet eye over Ruan, who looked not much older than Yseult in the enveloping nightwear. 'It weren't your fault about the cottage at Pencarne getting damaged by the weather. Act of nature, and we'll have to make the best of it. Now eat your supper afore it gets cold.'

Ruan uncovered the dishes and found a chicken stew with small airy dumplings, and for sweet a custard mousse that looked delicious. She smiled at Jancey. 'Thank you for cooking supper for us. It looks very tasty.'

'Mr. Talgarth gave orders for something hot and substantial, so eat it all up.' The housekeeper departed, and Yseult shot a wide-eyed look at Ruan.

'I don't much care for that woman,' she said. 'And I don't like dumplings.'

'Eat a couple, they're good for the sniffles.' Ruan smiled encouragingly. 'Downstairs you were telling me how much you looked forward to staying here. Have you changed your mind? If so, I'm sure we could get lodgings in Pencarne village.'

'Oh no.' Yseult started to eat her supper. 'I want to stay here very much – it's just that I get a bit nervous at night, and Jancey isn't very friendly. I suppose Eduard keeps her on because she's a good cook.'

'Yes, I suppose he does.' Ruan bent her head to hide the

dimple in her cheek, for she couldn't help being amused by Yseult's grown-up airs. 'This stew is nice and warming, isn't it?'

'Mmm. Do you suppose Eduard will come up and say goodnight to us?'

'I hope not!'

Yseult looked at Ruan and laughed. 'I believe you're shy of him.'

'I'm shy of being seen in bed like this by any man. He wouldn't dare—' Ruan broke off and bit her lip. She knew there were many things Eduard Talgarth would dare, and the very thought of being seen by him in plaits and flannelette was enough to make her want to hide under the covers. Those devil-blue eyes of his would never stop smiling!

She was all on thorns, and every movement outside in the gallery seemed to sound like his footsteps. It was such a relief when Jancey came for the depleted tray and brought a verbal message from him. He wished them a comfortable night and would wait until the morning to give them the messages sent by Yseult's father from London. He had, also, something special to tell Miss Perry.

'Goodnight to you both.' Jancey rustled her way to the door, as lost in time as the house she served in her stiff dark dress, her silvery hair knotted at the nape of her neck, and a bunch of keys rattling on a chatelaine at her narrow waist. 'You have no need to be nervous of the ghost of the chateau. The master sleeps in the rooms that once belonged to Eduard le Valliante. It's the turret above the master suite that he's said to haunt.'

The door closed behind her, and the lamplight glimmered in the large eyes of the two girls as they looked at each other. 'He wouldn't be afraid,' Yseult whispered.

'No,' Ruan agreed, her dimple a small half-moon in her cheek. 'It would take more than a legend and a shadow to unnerve the master of the chateau. I wonder—?'

'What special thing he has to tell you in the morning?'

'Yes. Ruan couldn't help but wonder who he had seen

in London apart from Hugh Strathern. 'Shall I turn out the lamp?'

'If you must,' Yseult said nervously.

'Snuggle down and you'll be sound asleep in no time.' The lamp clicked out and in the darkness of the vast old room the sea far below took on a nearer sound. In a while someone could be heard limping – Medevil putting out the lights along the gallery. Then a horse whinnied and stamped in the stable, and foliage rustled against the stone walls of the chateau.

The place was two hundred years old and its legends were as much a part of St. Avrell as the granite cliffs on which it was built, and the wide moors surrounding it. It was a house built for a large family, but all that remained was a single man, his few faithful servants, and the horse he rode along the mottled sands when the sun was setting. He had once warned her that if she ever came to Cornwall she would learn what manner of man he was. But she knew already – he was bold, and he was a little bad, and lonely enough to marry just for the companionship. Perhaps in all his wanderings he had never found someone he could really love.

A golden scatter of early morning sunlight was in the room when she awoke. The clock told her how early it was, but almost at once she wanted to rise, to look about her, to become acquainted with the chateau.

She slipped out of bed and took her clothes into the bathroom so she wouldn't wake Yseult, who would sleep on for another hour or two. It would do her good, for yesterday she had looked as if she were catching a cold. Ruan herself felt active and restless, and after a wash she put on her sweater and glen-plaid skirt, made the best of her rainmarked casuals, and let herself out of the bedroom as quietly as possible.

Last night she had been too confused by the events brought about by the rainstorm to take much heed of her surroundings, but this morning she noticed the dark, historic

Armada wood of the staircase, curving down to the hall where the chairs and the prayer-stool were still grouped about the dead fire. She heard in the silence the soft boom of the sea, and saw the sun striking through long windows at the end of the hall. She made for the sun and passed on her way a brassbound ship's clock, and an oriental vase with petals fallen from a cluster of roses. Red roses, adding to the bouquet of the chateau, a mingling of weathered stone, of polished wood, and the salt tang of the ocean. The strong and virile Atlantic beating for ever at the rocks below.

Ruan felt the beating of her heart as she stepped into the large garden of the chateau, which rambled with a will of its own, past arbours and statues and nooks where birds perched upon seats of teak. Quite suddenly she came to a wall, with buds and briars glinting darkly against a scrambling mass of roses. She stood in wonderment, wanting to touch the scarlet cloak but afraid of the briars.

There was a small door and she tried it and entered the walled rose garden. It was entrancing and unexpected to find so lovely a place in the heart of the grounds. The scent was intoxicating, arising from bushes of tea-roses, smothered pergolas, and elegant damasks with a velvet swirling of petals. They grew in a passionate riot of colour, clusters and fountains of the most lovely flower on earth, the garden of a crusader who had come home after long wanderings to buy back from strangers the Talgarth heritage. This place of turrets against a windswept sky, a dream in reality.

Ruan lingered in the rose garden, where the dew still lay on the petals and small gold spiders drowsed in their webs. She wondered if the dark Talgarth came often to this romantic place. She had seen roses in the hall of the chateau, and a man who liked to work with his hands could be a man who tended roses and found them lovely.

Red roses for kindness ... entwined briars for star-crossed lovers.

She let herself out of the door at the opposite side of the

enclosure and found herself on a winding footpath. She followed it and came out upon the turf-covered cliffs that towered from the sea, where large waves were sweeping in over smaller waves, drowning them, their crests shot with sunshine so they gleamed like glass.

There was a bank of gorse and wild fuchsia that formed a soft, musky barrier where Ruan knelt to take in the scene below. The salty wind blew her hair about her slender face, and her lips were stung to coral, and she thought she saw a seal swimming among the breakers until, with a little gasp, she realized that it was a man. She and Yseult had been warned not to swim when the waves were high, but Eduard Talgarth seemed reckless himself of the strength and danger of the St. Avrell waters. He breasted the waves and his black head and lean body could be seen for a moment, then the waters covered him again and it seemed to Ruan that he would never emerge.

She held her breath as she awaited another glimpse of him. He was obviously a strong and seasoned swimmer, but what if he got caught in the undertow around those rocks? What if he knocked his head and never appeared again?

She knelt there, and the clamour of the ocean mingled with the bird cries as she tried to see beneath the froth on the glass waves. She searched for an upraised arm, the strip of navy briefs against the tanned limbs, the seal-blackness of his hair. Her anxiety grew as the minutes ticked by, and then clearly on the morning air she heard a deep-timbred voice singing, coming nearer all the time up the footpath where blackthorn grew, and columbine, and straggles of sea-pinks.

> Open the door, my hinny, my heart.
> Open the door, my own darling ...

Ruan jumped to her feet as he appeared over the headland and was outlined a moment against the gold and blue of the morning sky. His black hair was wet and tousled; he wore a turtle-neck sweater of white and narrow dark slacks that lengthened his legs even more. A pair of damp swimming briefs swung in his hand, and he stopped singing as he caught sight of her, the words 'my own darling' on his lips as he stared at Ruan.

'Hullo there!' he exclaimed. 'You're an early riser.'

'So are you.' She was confused by the look of him; by the song he had been singing, and by her anxiety for a man who knew the sea too well to let it get the better of him. He had evidently swum underwater to a hidden cove and there he had dressed.

'I'm used to an early swim. I used to dive over the side of the *Pandora* and swim in the peacock waters. They look so warm, and yet it's amazing how cool they can be.' He came through the gorse to her side and before she knew his intention he took something from a strand of her hair. A rose petal, like a patch of red velvet in his hand. 'You've been in my rose garden, eh?'

'I – I hope you don't mind?'

'Mind?' His blue eyes looked quizzically into hers. 'You seem to think me a bit of a bluebeard, Ruan. None of my doors are locked against you. Did it come as a pleasant surprise to find the enchanted garden of the ogre?'

He stood grinning at her, too blue-eyed, too sea-clean to frighten her this morning. Fright had come while he was down there, and she gave him an annoyed look for breaking through her defences. 'Isn't it rather unusual for a man of the sea to have a green thumb?' she asked.

He looked at his hand and rubbed his thumb against the velvety rose petal. 'I've always liked the primeval feel of wood, metal, or growing things. I had ambitions to be a sculptor, but it would have taken longer that way to make money.' His eyes held hers. 'Are you shocked by so mercenary a statement?'

'Not in the circumstances,' she had to admit. His hands were lean, hard, tanned by the sun of the tropics. 'I've heard that the chateau fell into the hands of strangers and you had to get it back for the Talgarths.'

'At present there's only the one,' he drawled, and she

followed his gaze to the turrets of the chateau, the conical tower at the side, with a gallery over the arched doorway. The lacy ironwork of the narrow windows, and the ship's pennant blowing in the wind above the fable-like structure that would stand another century because it was built of Cornish stone.

'The standard is off the *Pandora*, my favourite ship,' he said. 'She's in dry dock at Port Perryn and I may one day sail her again. Who knows?'

Ruan detected a note of nostalgia in his voice – and something almost reckless, as if there would be nothing to hold him to the land if he failed to make the chateau a family house once again. Did she realize that it took more than the possession of a house to make a home, this man who looked as if he had been ruthless towards the women met in his travels who might have loved him? And then he slowly smiled at her and she was uncertain of her thoughts of him. His mouth seemed almost gentle, and yet a moment before it had looked quite grim.

'Each one of us is a divided personality,' he said. 'We each have a star to follow, but the course is not always set in a straight line. It's like searching for an uncharted island, you can only follow the map a certain part of the way and then you're on your own. Often you never find the island, but if you do it seems like heaven – until a storm strikes.'

She stared at him and felt the quick beating of her heart. 'You said last night that you had something special to tell me. It's about Tarquin, isn't it?'

'Yes. He had to see Hugh Strathern for a final checkup, and Hugh pronounced him fit and asked if he was off to make a film. Powers replied that he was going to America – to see his wife.'

There was a tense silence, broken only by the seabirds and the far downbeat of the waves, rhythmic, urgent, like the pain that caught at Ruan and then ebbed away to a dull ache. Knowing Tarquin had been a banquet she had never thought to attend – now the table was cleared, the candles were out, the wine was cold and forgotten in the loving cup. She shivered, and then felt the warm grip of a hand pulling her away from the cliff edge.

'Come and have breakfast with me.' Talgarth spoke crisply. 'I cook it myself in the studio I have in that witch-peaked tower. All the ingredients are there, and for a seaman with a green thumb I cook up a fairly decent meal.'

They walked side by side through the dewy gorse and she preceded him along the winding path that led to the rose garden. She was aware of his tallness behind her, of his gaze upon her as the wind blew her skirt above her knees and whipped her hair into a loop about her throat. She felt that odd irrational urge to break into a run, and he must have sensed it, for he gave a laugh.

'Ruan, you're just like your name,' he taunted. 'You're always running away, even when we seem to find a bit of sympathy to share. You don't like me, and I have a favour to ask of you.'

'A favour?' She swung round from the door in the rose garden wall, and her eyes appealed to him not to ask anything of her. The giving and taking of favours bestowed a certain intimacy and she shied from any sort of closeness to Eduard Talgarth.

His lip quirked as he reached out and pushed open the door of the rose garden, so that once again she was surrounded by the red ramblers, the pastel damasks, and the entwining briars. But this time the dark Talgarth was there to share the beauty of the roses, their intoxicating scent and their symbolism.

'What favour do you imagine I'd ask of you? From the look in your eyes it's something too dire for words. Ruan,' he laughed again, 'it isn't a kiss, nor a proposal of marriage. Did you think it was?'

'Of course not!'

'Then why do you look so apprehensive? You could slap me for taking a kiss, and you can always say no if I ask you to marry me.'

'Please stop the teasing and tell me what you mean by

a favour.'

'Teasing, eh?' He cupped a rose in his hand, honey-pink against the deep tan of his skin. 'Don't you think I'd like to kiss you, Ruan Perry? Other men have wanted to.'

'You no doubt find it amusing to talk in this vein, Mr. Talgarth, and I believe you're curious. You'd like to find out why Tarquin enjoyed my company, and why Hugh Strathern wants to see me again. I've never kissed Hugh, if you're curious on that score.'

'But matters went a bit further with the charming actor, eh?'

'I – I don't want to discuss it.' Her fingers clenched a rose, then she gave a pained gasp as a thorn stabbed her thumb. At once Eduard caught hold of her hand and before she could stop him he bent his head and drew out the poison. All the time he looked at her with those magnetic blue eyes, and she was aware of the primitive forces in him, the ability to shock with a kindness or a cruelty. There was no middle way for him; none of the sophistication that made other men seem less formidable. If a snake had bitten her, he would have acted in the same way.

'The rose can be dangerous,' he said quietly. 'I had to have a finger lanced a fortnight ago. There, it didn't hurt being touched by my lips, did it?'

She flushed, for he had made the incident seem like a moment of lovemaking. 'Th – thank you.' She drew her hand from his and looked at the little mark so she wouldn't have to look at him. 'Now I can't refuse you a favour, can I?'

'Not even if it were a proposal?'

Her shocked eyes lifted to his, and he laughed outright, a bold sound with a lash of mockery in it. 'Don't swoon, Ruan. I might look a bit of a pirate, with Cornish right-of-wreck instincts not far below the surface, but I'd no more salvage a broken candy cask than I'd want a girl in love with another man. There'd be nothing in it, either way, and Talgarth likes to strike a warmer bargain.'

Ruan slowly smiled, for this was the Talgarth she understood, the tough trader who would have felt himself well rewarded if Charme St. Cyr had agreed to marry him. He smiled with her, a quizzical glint in his eyes, and opened the door that led out of the rose garden. Soon they came in sight of the conical tower in which he had his studio, and as they entered through the arched door and mounted some winding stairs to the room, a large cat brushed past her legs and she gave a gasp of surprise and found Eduard close to her on that narrow stairway.

'It's only Tinker. He used to sail with us on the *Pandora* and like Medevil he came home with me when I left the sea. He goes to the attic under the tower to hunt for mice.' A hand enclosed her elbow, so strong and yet curiously sensitive, as if each nerve was vibrant with life. As if the shape of bones was more beautiful to him than their covering. As if each petal on the rose was more lovely than the complete flower. As if in wood or metal he sought to create the flesh and the petal.

He was a strange, complex being ... an adventurer and a dreamer, and Ruan felt a sense of wonderment as she entered his studio. The air was filled with the tang of wood shavings, and the benches were littered with tools and carvings, and a bronzed head. Strong, almost cruel, a flick of a smile on the bold lips ... a self-sculpture!

'Look at it, pick it up, if you want to.' He strolled to the other side of the circular room, where there was a cupboard, a small brass stove, and cooking utensils.

She studied the head and knew it to be a bold work of art, yet it lacked something that made her turn and look at Eduard, as if for inspiration. He cast her a glance as he broke eggs into a pan and lit the gas jets of the stove ... she met eyes blue as daylight, with lashes dark as night, and knew that was why the carving was dead in comparison to the man.

The thing about Eduard Talgarth that shook a woman was that he was so intensely alive, from his black shock of hair to his broad shoulders, down to his firmly planted feet, as if even yet he stood on the deck of a sailing ship.

'Bacon with the eggs, and fried bread?' he asked.

She nodded and realized how hungry she was. 'You're clever with your hands,' she said. 'This is very good.'

He shrugged. 'I need a more beautiful model ... I need the winged look. Do you like that seagull?'

'Oh yes.' It was in applewood, lighter, as if carved with a more loving touch. 'You like the wild things, don't you?'

'You sound surprised.' He turned to look at her as the eggs sizzled merrily. 'I'm more in touch with the wild than the tame ... I thought you knew, guessed it, at least.'

'It isn't always easy to guess things about you, Mr. Talgarth.' She stroked a wing of the seagull. 'I haven't a clue to this favour you want to ask of me.'

'Haven't you?' He flicked a look over Ruan in her short plaid skirt and lavender sweater, took in her wind tangled hair and her eyes that changed so elusively from grey to violet. 'I believe anyone but you would have guessed ten minutes ago. I want you to model for me.'

She looked at him a stunned half-minute, while he transferred the eggs to a plate and laid slices of bacon in the pan. On the other jet a coffee pot was bubbling, filling the room with the aroma of really good coffee, the sort that didn't come out of a tin. 'Why should you want me for a model?' she gasped. 'I'm not beautiful.'

'No, *liebchen*.' He spoke lazily. 'You aren't like diamonds, iced champagne, and silver orchids.'

'Charme?'

'All those things.'

'Poor man, not to have got her to the chateau as your model, or your wife.' Ruan gave a shaky laugh. 'And what am I, your substitute model?'

'You are wild violets, Ruan, a running stream in the woods, a piskie pin.' He swung right round, his heavy eyelids lifted and she saw the hint of a tempest in his blue eyes. His scrutiny was that of a ship's captain, a pirate of the high seas, a man who had met many women and knew her for the most innocent of them.

'I'd like to sculpt you,' he said. 'As a haunted young

Undine waiting for her prince.'

'No!' The word broke from her. 'I refuse ... utterly.'

'You're being rather childish.'

'And you're being cruel!'

'Ah, you think me cruel, Ruan?'

'Yes. You want to capture the haunting and the hurt that's in me.'

'I admit you have a certain look that I find intriguing, but it's something you were born with and has nothing to do with the pangs of adolescence.' He quirked that black eyebrow as he spoke, and a wicked little peak formed above his left eye. 'You've a lot to learn about men, Ruan. You've a devil of a lot to learn about me.'

Suddenly the bacon was smoking and he turned away to attend to the food. She watched him and felt a smarting in her eyes. She blinked away the tears, for it would be mortifying to cry in front of this man who had never really loved anything except his ships and the ocean and being clever with his hands. He wanted those hands to create a girl of stone to match his heart of stone. All right! She would be his model for the Undine who could never cause him heartache.

'When would you like me to start modelling for you?' she asked.

He dished up the food, poured the coffee, and pulled out a chair at a gateleg table for her. Outside the tower studio birds were whistling in the trees and there was a rattle of a milk van coming up the hill. 'Tomorrow, if you're quite sure you want to go through with it,' he said. 'I never start anything unless I mean to finish it.'

'It will repay you for your hospitality to Yseult and myself.' She bent her head to her plate. 'You like to strike a good bargain.'

'Do you think I bargain for everything, Ruan?'

'Don't you, Mr. Talgarth? I believe you think you can even buy a wife.'

'I know I could, if I chose to. He laughed. 'As a well-seasoned traveller I can assure you that I've seen a woman bought for a pearl, or a flock of goats. How does that strike you?'

She glanced up and found his eyes teasing her over the rim of his coffee cup. 'If I had to be bought, I'd prefer to be bought with a pearl. Anyway this is England, not some barbaric corner of the world.'

'Don't you believe it happens in this civilized country of ours?'

His tone was ironical, and she bit her lip, remembering Charme's determined salesmanship of herself to the highest bidder. 'I prefer to believe in love, Mr. Talgarth. I can't visualize any real, lasting happiness without it.'

'Did it make you happy?'

'For a while I was very happy.'

'You caught a glimpse of heaven, eh?'

'If you want to put it that way.'

'Maybe one day, Ruan, your eyes will be opened to the real thing.'

'It was real,' she said fiercely.

'A dream seems real, then we awake and the dream gives way to reality. It's much more satisfying in the end to grasp reality rather than a dream figure.'

'Oh, you wouldn't understand!'

'Wouldn't I?' He chewed bacon and egg, and looked amused. 'I wonder why you think so?'

'Would you believe anything I told you about Katmandu, when you've been there and I haven't?'

'Meaning I have to fall in love before I dare be wise about it?' His eyes were a brilliant blue as he dabbed a check-patterned napkin against his lips. 'More coffee, Ruan?'

'Please.'

'I'm glad my coffee pleases you.'

'I'm very thirsty.'

'You're asking to be spanked, young lady.' His eyes gleamed as he handed her the cup. 'One of these fine days—'

'You'd have to catch me first, Mr. Talgarth.'

'I intend to,' he drawled. 'You'll be spanked, or kissed.'

Her heart missed a beat when he said that, but when she looked at him he was sugaring his coffee and a ray of sunshine slanted across his face and made his expression unreadable. Such a strong, dark, Celtic face ... it sent a tingle all the way down her spine, for it was the face of a man who kept his word!

CHAPTER NINE

THE roar of the incoming tide, the great swell of the waves, the crash as they climbed the rocks and broke in a great scatter of spray. This was the music of the chateau of St. Avrell, the heartbeat of it, and Ruan never went down to the shore without remembering the boy who long ago had hunted here for shells and thought the rocks like knights at their vigil.

It was strange, as if no matter where she ran she would never escape him. And when she listened to the waves she seemed to hear his voice. 'Do you think I don't get frightened, dear nymph? Do you think I want the pain of saying good-bye to you?'

But there had been no pain for him when he had said good-bye to her ... he had said it to a stranger, and now all this ocean separated them.

She ran along the shore pursued by bird calls. She mustn't think about anything but this holiday, which had taken such a strange turn. Not only was she a guest at the chateau, but each day she posed for the figure of Undine, and to her relief Eduard allowed Yseult to be present at the sittings. It was much like sitting for an artist, except that he worked in clay, using his mobile fingers to shape her features and the contours of her slim figure reclining on a rock brought up from the beach to the courtyard of his studio.

There had been the question of what to wear. Though Jem Lovibond had salvaged most of their belongings, Eduard had found her dresses too up-to-date and said she must wear something that clung softly to her figure and had the look of sea mist floating around her.

It was upon his orders that Medevil carried a large sandalwood box down from one of the attics, and when it was opened both girls caught their breath in surprise and delight. It was full of silken things that would have pulled through a gold ring.

Ruan felt compelled to look at Eduard, tall by the mantelpiece, a cigar between his teeth, and he half-smiled and made her wonder if there had been a special girl in his life, someone exquisite, on whom such lovely Eastern silks would look stunning.

'There was a planter on one of the coffee islands,' he said, smoke drifting upwards past the glints in his eyes. 'He ordered a trousseau for his bride-to-be, but when we arrived at the island in the *Pandora* one of the plantation houseboys came running on board to tell me not to unload the cargo ordered by his master. His girl had written to say she was marrying someone else; she couldn't face life on an island after all. Somehow the sandalwood box and its contents remained on the *Pandora* until I sailed her home to Cornwall. You should find something there, Ruan, to wear for me.'

She flushed at the way he put it and knelt by the box of silks, into which Yseult was delving with all the carelessness of a child. She didn't understand how sad it really was that a lonely man should want to lavish so much loveliness on a girl, only to receive a cool letter saying she didn't care enough to share his island.

'Isn't this gorgeous?' Yseult had draped herself in a shimmering length of sea-green silk.

'That isn't the way to wear a *sari*.' Cigar clenched in his teeth, Eduard took hold of Yseult and with a couple of deft movements of his hands he draped the silk correctly. 'There, now you look as pretty as a temple dancer.'

Yseult smiled and danced around the room, her gay young reflection caught and held a dozen times in the gilded mirrors of the *salon*. 'Wouldn't you like me to model for you?' she asked.

'You wouldn't sit still long enough. I'd finish up with a blob of something looking four ways at once, with legs and arms all over the place.' He drew lazily on his cigar.

'We'll wait till you're grown up and have a little more repose.'

'Like Ruan?' Yseult shot a look of mischief at her young chaperone, who with her switch of hair to her waist was admiring a length of gossamer tulle.

'I could make a sort of Greek dress with this,' she said. 'Isn't it a beautiful colour, like a silvery grey cloud with tinges of pink and flame?'

Eduard didn't say anything and she glanced at him for his reaction. Her heart gave a funny little leap, for his eyes were so intensely alive in his craggy face, like two blue flames burning her as he studied her from across the room. She couldn't tell what he was thinking. Perhaps that she wouldn't look half so attractive as the girls who danced in the courtyards of Eastern pagodas.

He smiled lazily. 'Yes, wear that. Make the dress so it has panels of odd lengths, to give the effect of rags and tatters. Undine was a waif of the seashore, in love with a prince from the castle. She shouldn't look too sophisticated ... somehow enchantment has a sort of innocence about it. Those who possess the real thing are often unaware of the fact.'

'I like the story of Undine ... it seems to suit Ruan.' Yseult set the radiogram in motion and a lovely piece by Debussy put an end to conversation until it died softly away. Eduard then rang for Medevil and told him to bring a bottle of wine to the *salon*. 'It isn't often I have guests and we should celebrate the occasion,' he said.

Medevil nodded and smiled at Yseult in her sea-green drapery. He looked pleased that his '*maître*' was being entertained by his young lady guests.

It would be lonely here a good deal of the time, Ruan realized. The chateau was remote from other houses, and Eduard had said himself that he had lost contact with the people he had known in his youth. He had sailed away to distant shores when he was nineteen, and for a long time the chateau had stood empty, unlived in by the stranger who had bought it. Out of the blue Eduard had returned to Cornwall, rich enough to buy back the family home, a sea trading merchant with his friends scattered across the Indies. Planters and sea captains. Men of adventure like himself ... whom he might rejoin if the chateau remained for him but a lonely house on a cliff top.

But this evening there was music. The lamps were alight and the lonely sea and the moors were shut out by long brocade curtains. Soon Medevil returned with the wine and the cobwebs around the neck of the bottle made it appear as if it had been in the cellar since the wild old smuggling days.

'Don't wrinkle your nose,' Eduard said to Yseult, as he poured the wine into a carafe of fine glass, with the tiny faces of fauns, and tiny grapes and leaves etched in a tracery of silver. 'Wine is all the better for being mature, and this batch was put down in my grandfather's time, straight out of a French vineyard. The Talgarths were county in those days. My grandmother used to give large parties and the banquet table in the dining-room used to seat a hundred people. They'd dance all night, breakfast on eggs, bacon and champagne, and then ride out across the moors to whip up an appetite for more dining and dancing.'

'It must have been super, with all the chandeliers aglow, and musicians playing up in the gallery.' Yseult's eyes were shining. 'Couldn't you revive it all, Eduard?'

He shook his head, but for a moment Ruan seemed to glimpse a wistfulness in his eyes, as if he had hoped for some return of the old happy days. But Charme had rejected him, and Ruan had now seen the portrait of his grandmother in the morning-room where she used to write her letters and her party invitations. A smiling, pert-faced creature, with a mass of fair hair and huge blue eyes, jewels glinting against her creamy neck, she was the woman who had made a large hole in the Talgarth fortune. Her son – Eduard's father – had inherited her love of a good time and company, and in the end the chateau and the family jewels had gone to pay off his

164

gambling debts. His son had had to buy back his inheritance.

He poured the wine into small glasses that matched the carafe and handed one to each of the girls. Yseult was thrilled. 'May I say the toast?' she asked him. 'Please let me!'

'Of course you may.' He gave her a bow that revealed his Breton blood. 'I rarely have company, and two such pretty guests have a crusty seaman at their command.'

'I don't think you're a bit crusty,' Yseult protested. 'You're as gallant as that Eduard of long ago.'

'You're very charming to say so.' He smiled, but he was not teasing Yseult. There was no devilish glint in his eye; no wicked arch to his eyebrow. His gaze was gentle as it dwelt upon the red-gold hair of his younger guest, a leggy schoolgirl as yet, but who in a year or two would be grown up enough to turn a man's head with her green-eyed smile. As the daughter of his friend she would often come here; as a man lonely for company he would welcome her.

Ruan was a little shocked by her thoughts, yet they persisted. Yseult made no secret of her fondness for him, and he wouldn't be the first mature man to take a girl-bride.

'And now that toast before the bubbles go out of the wine,' he said to her.

Yseult gave him a curtsy. 'Wine was meant to be, or there would be no grapes on the vines. Love was meant to be, or there would be no women. There!'

This time he did quirk his left eyebrow, and then he raised his wine glass, first to Yseult, and more slowly to Ruan, his eyes brilliant, daring, holding for her a little spark of mockery and not a hint of the gentleness he showed the younger girl. She sipped her wine and turned to study a collection of rare objects he had brought back from his travels and kept in a treasure table. Pieces of jade of unusual colours, a tiny pagoda carved from ivory, an idol with jewelled eyes, and amulets inscribed with tiny letters.

She glanced at her scarab ring with the tiny lettering under the wing ... instead of happiness it seemed as if the ring had brought only misfortune. It was as if some spell lay upon it ... was it possible that a thing so charming could be unlucky.

'Admiring my jade?'

She gave a start as Eduard came to her side. 'Yes – it's very beautiful, and I had no idea it was so vari-coloured.'

'These things are very evocative. They remind me of river festivals and flower boats, of gongs and temple ruins, and pools of golden carp.' He opened the glass top of the table and lifted from its bed a spray of cherry-blossom carved from jade, translucent and delicate as a breath of air. 'This is many years old. Do you see, it has a clip at the back so it can be worn in the hair. Cherry-blossom was the flower of love at the old courts of China, and this pin might have been worn by a Mandarin's sweetheart as she fluttered about him, bringing his tea, soothing him with an ivory fan, or listening at his feet as he read verses to her.'

Ruan glanced at him, for he always surprised her when he talked like this, revealing his love of delicate trifles and his knowledge of old traditions. 'Do you wish women were still like that?' she asked.

'Obedient to a man's every whim?' he drawled. 'It would be rather pleasant to have a loving slave, but I prefer frankly a girl with spirit who enjoys the fireworks of an argument. Who gives me hell ... and promises heaven.'

He replaced the jade, and took from the case a pair of fine chains with a little gold Buddha attached to each one. 'Please accept this as a keepsake.' He dropped one of the chains into Ruan's hand, then he strolled across to Yseult and fastened the companion chain around her wrist. He did it gallantly, while Ruan stood alone by the table with her fingers clenching slowly on the little Buddha – god of repose and reflection.

'Oh, Eduard, it's lovely!' Yseult flung her arms about his neck and stood on tiptoe to kiss his lean brown cheek.

'You're my favourite man ... please wait for me to grow up, or I shall go into a nunnery!'

He laughed as she toyed with the wrist-chain. 'When you are older, Yseult, I shall remind you of this evening and you'll laugh to remember the young girl who pledged herself to a nunnery. By then you'll have all you dream of.'

'Do dreams come true?' she asked him wistfully.

'For the young in heart, my gilly, and sometimes for those who know the need for love because they've never had it. And now it's time for you and Ruan to trot off to bed.'

'Already?' she protested.

'It's past ten o'clock and you look sleepy.' He glanced at Ruan and a smile lingered at the corner of his mouth though his eyes were a trifle sombre. 'Do you both sleep well under the roof of the chateau? You mustn't let our ghost worry you. According to legend he only haunts a Talgarth, and I occupy the rooms where he's said to wander. He's just a lonely exile, rather like myself.'

'But Cornwall is your home—'

'Cornwall is where I was born, but no place is home unless the heart is there. And now I'll bid you both goodnight – if you'd like some hot milk I'll tell Medevil to bring it up to you.'

Yseult wrinkled her nose. 'Hot milk reminds me of school!'

'Heaven forbid!' He was now lighting one of his thin cigars, as if he meant to smoke alone in the *salon* or to take a stroll as far as the walled garden where the night air would be redolent of the rambling roses.

'Thank you for the keepsake,' said Ruan awkwardly.

'You're welcome.' His eyes seemed to hold teasing glints through the smoke of his cigar. 'It's said to bring good fortune to a house to give of its treasures to a stranger – do you feel a stranger still?'

She didn't know how to reply to him. There had been too many times in her life when she had felt the outsider, and a look, a gesture could reawaken the feeling. Giving her a trinket had been but a gesture. She hadn't wanted him to fasten it about her wrist, yet the cool manner of his giving had reminded her vividly of the days of her adolescence, when Charme had been made so much more of; when a gift to herself had been but a tiresome duty so far as her stepfather was concerned.

She wanted nothing from anyone, if it could not be given freely, but already she had thanked Eduard for the trinket, and the firm jut of his chin was always a warning not to tangle with him unless you were well prepared for the fight. Tonight she felt curiously defenceless, and when he took a sudden step close to her she felt as if her knees would give way.

'What's the matter?' he demanded in a low voice. 'Have I done something to hurt you? Surely not, Ruan. You're immune from what I can inflict on you. I'm just that tiresome Cornishman with the odd ability to read your mind. I know right now what you're thinking.'

'You can't know!'

'But I do know, Ruan. You're thinking about Avendon and the humility you were taught there. Always to take a back seat, to sit in the shadows and watch the drama and desire of other people's lives. Then you found a little drama of your own, but the curtain came down on it, and right now you're feeling hurt and rebellious. You don't want to sit out in the cold any more ... you want to be loved, don't you, Ruan?'

'How dare you?' She fought the strange weakness in her legs and backed away from his tall figure and his dark face, his eyes narrowed speculatively against the smoke of his cigar. 'Yseult, I'm off to bed! Are you coming?'

'I was just having another peek in the bride's box. Ruan, will you make me a dress out of some of this gorgeous silk?'

'Yes, my dear, tomorrow.'

'Good night, Ruan,' Eduard said deliberately. 'Sweet dreams.'

'I—' She wanted to protest that she hated him ... it

168

was shocking to be so transparent to a man, as if she had no secret that was safe from him.

'Don't say it,' he drawled. 'You might regret it.'

'You're incorrigible!' She tossed her head, turned on her heel and marched out of the room. She was halfway up the stairs before Yseult caught up with her.

'You've been quarrelling with him again,' the younger girl accused. 'I don't know how you can!'

'It's easy,' said Ruan. 'He's the most presumptuous devil I've ever had the misfortune to meet. He's been a ship's captain so long that he thinks he can boss everyone as he did his long-suffering crew. Poor men! They must have thought they had Captain Bligh on board!'

Yseult giggled, 'You're funny, Ruan.'

'I'm glad you appreciate my humour, only I'm not being funny on purpose. The sooner Rock Haven is set to rights the better I shall like it. We can then pack up and leave this place – and that man.'

'He was kind enough to give us a bangle each. I love mine, with its little gold idol. I shall wear it in bed.' Yseult admired her wrist-chain. 'He was going to give me a ring, but I expect he'll save it for when I'm older. It's very significant for a man to give a girl a ring – though I've heard that in Spain a bangle is a love token. It would be a thrill if Eduard meant one of us for his future bride.'

With deliberation Ruan dropped her own chain on the dressing-table. The tiny idol gleamed in the lamplight, reminding her that anger was foolish and that reflection brought wisdom. Oh, but the man was so annoying . . . not even Charme with her pointed remarks could arouse the spitfire in Ruan as did that tall devil with eyes so blue and deep it was like drowning in them when he looked at her.

Her mind was made up; as soon as Jem brought word that the cottage was fit to live in again, she and Yseult would pack their belongings and leave the chateau. But in the meantime she had to make the best of a situation she found tense and disturbing.

As she undressed she became aware that Yseult had

gone to bed in her own room tonight, though she had left the communicating door ajar. 'Good night, Yseult,' she called out. 'Sleep well.'

'Good night,' Yseult mumbled.

Ruan sighed and slipped into her own enormous bed. How did you explain to the young that antagonisms were as natural as affections; that try as she might she couldn't feel at ease with Eduard Talgarth? He made her feel untried and unworldly, as if her love for Tarquin had been but a step into womanhood instead of the most profound happening in her life. She had nothing to cling to if she couldn't believe that Tarquin had loved her in return. His dear nymph, sharing with him those sunlit hours on the river Avon.

When she switched out the lamp her fingers came in contact with the little idol, and she made a vow. She would try to be friends with Eduard. There were times when she found him interesting, especially when he talked about the arts and crafts of the Eastern lands and revealed the side of him that was cultured, even rather gentle.

She was smiling a little as she drifted off to sleep ... gentle was perhaps a word to smile at when applied to the master of the chateau.

When sittings for Undine were over for the day, the two girls were free to enjoy the chateau and its surroundings. They discovered a hard tennis court in spanking condition and played for fun, until their host came along and challenged them to a game. He took on the pair of them and had such a swift forearm swing with the racquet that he had them diving about the court until they were laughingly exhausted and had to be revived with tall cool drinks.

The jingle was also at their command, and Eduard often drove them to see the romantic haunts of Cornwall. They visited the castle ruins of Tintagel, where whispers of the old legends seemed to linger in the air and where at twilight the old ghosts might wander, the swirling of waves around the sharp dark rocks that guarded the ancient ruins.

They saw the little church of the six virtues, and Ruan noticed the smile hovering about Eduard's lips as they studied the figures in the stained glass window. 'Who would you choose?' she asked unexpectedly.

'Hope,' he said. 'She must surely possess all the other virtues.'

'Faith and charity,' Ruan murmured. 'Justice, praise and joy. A woman like that would have to be an angel. I'm sure you don't expect to find for yourself an angel, Mr. Talgarth.'

'The name is Eduard.'

'Eduard,' she said obediently.

He gazed down at her in the spangling of coloured light from the window. 'Don't you think an angel would have me?'

'If she loved you.' Then Ruan drew away from him and went to look at the stone knight who had caught Yseult's attention.

As they drove around the countryside, they were noticed by the people who lived in the moorland cottages. Curtains twitched at the tiny windows and curious eyes watched them go jingling by. Everyone knew that the roving Talgarth had returned, maybe to settle down and take a bride. Would it be one of the young ladies with long, wind-blown hair ... it wasn't quite right for them to be sharing a house with a bachelor, but there had always been a dash of the devil in the Talgarth men!

Speculation was in the wind, carrying across the moors from one cottage to another, and if some of the curiosity reached Eduard, he revealed it only in the deepset twinkle in his eyes.

They drove over the moors to Dozemary Pool, more of a tarn with its still water and the ravens cawing in the stillness. The legend said that from here King Arthur had been rowed to Avalon, the final resting place of Celtic chieftains. Here his great sword had sunk with a last flash of lightning beneath the water of the tarn, and only the ravens and the reeds made any sound as the two girls stood there, awestruck, with Eduard.

'Come!' He took each girl around the waist and the trio hastened away from the haunted pool and scrambled into the jingle with laughter and relief.

'Your Cornwall is very eerie in places,' said Yseult.

'Aye, it's a subtle place with a beauty altogether strange. It's the lover of the sea, whose sons are at once masters of the waves and yet the ocean's loving slaves. You must both come sailing with me in the *Halcyone*, the small sloop I keep in the bay under the chateau cliffs. She sails like a witch.'

'I was hoping you'd ask us to go sailing with you.'

'Were you, my gilly?' He whistled the pony to a trot and as the jingle carried them over the moorland road the wind tousled Eduard's black hair and stung the girls' cheeks with colour. The sky overhead was a wide arch of silvery blue, and here and there on the moors stood wind-bent trees and splashes of Cornish balm and gold-tipped gorse.

Yes, thought Ruan, this land's beauty was wild and un-tameable, and the subtle charm of the people captivated you before you were aware. The sea was always within sound, beyond a ridge of cliffs, or caught as in a frame at the bottom of a hilly road, its salty tang mingling with the scents of gorse and balm.

Beauty . . . and at the same time danger, for more than one ship had broken her back upon the rocks of this coast-line, where the luring song of a mermaid seemed to echo in the wind.

Constantine Bay was a picturesque place with its sand towans, and there Eduard told their fortunes in the sand, using his whip-handle and telling them such absurd things that their laughter startled the gulls, the pretty beggars of the scraps left from their lunch of meat pasties.

'Tamarisks.' His eyes were upon them as they swayed in the sea breeze. 'They remind me of the tropics, of walls so sunlit that they took each shadow and etched it into a picture.'

'I believe you would like to go back there and be a lotus-eater, like Gauguin.' Yseult sat near to him, with her knees encircled by her arms.

'He wasn't that entirely, Yseult. He was a primitive, seeking truth beyond the sophistications we have come to regard as necessary. He struck through to the roots of longing deep inside each one of us and created an art almost childlike and yet at the same time as old as creation. He painted people stripped of their finery, which in the end only becomes cobwebs.'

Ruan listened as she stood with her feet in the surf, she watched an oyster-catcher flying low over the water, and she felt again that if Eduard found nothing to hold him to his hard-won heritage he would return to those islands that lay like jewels beyond her reach. She could only imagine their wonder and their peace.

'Look.' He was on his feet in a single supple movement. 'A seal grooming itself on that rock out there!'

'Isn't there a legend that mermaids turn themselves into seals?' Ruan turned her head to look at him, and as his blue eyes flashed over her, taking in her wind-tangled, surf-wet figure, a tingle as from a magnetic charge seemed to run through her. This was a man who had lived on pagan islands and she had a vivid mental picture of him plucking a girl out of the surf – laughing, joyous – and carrying her to a thatched house on stilts.

'You look a mermaid yourself with your dress clinging to your knees, and your hair like a tail.'

'Thanks for the compliment!'

'I'm not being funny.' His drawl was strangely soft. 'Mermaids are creatures of allurement, and sailors are said to be more susceptible to their strange appeal than other men.'

Ruan didn't know what to make of that remark, but she wanted to look away from him – casually – as if she didn't notice how the sea and the sun combined to bring out all that was primitively attractive in the man. His skin was brown in the neck opening of his shirt, and black was his hair, like iron, and broad were the shoulders that had never bowed beneath the tough burdens his life had imposed upon him.

It came as a relief when with a loud splash the seal dived off its perch and swam underwater with a swiftness no human being could match. 'The mermaid is off to her undersea palace,' Ruan laughed, a trifle breathlessly.

'To meet Prince Huldebrand.' Yseult gave a pirouette, her bright hair streaming out from her shoulders. 'This is turning out to be the best holiday I've ever had. Can we go to Camelford tomorrow, where King Arthur had his palace?'

'Anything you wish, my gilly.' Eduard smiled and there was a deep blue light in his eyes that matched the brilliance of the sea ... the two blues burned together.

'You're a super man!' Then in a fit of shyness Yseult bent to pick up a convoluted shell, only to drop it the next instant as something wriggled out of it. It was a tiny crab, scuttling over the sands and diverting Ruan's attention to a pathetic huddle of grey feathers, up near one of the small caves in the cliffside. She went towards it and saw a gull crouched there as if in hiding with a broken wing. Knowing gulls to be notoriously cruel towards injured members of their family, Ruan hurried over to this one to see what she could do to help.

As she was reaching up to the opening, the bird stirred out of its apathy, became alarmed and stabbed at her with its sharp beak.

'Ruan – ' Strong hands seized hold of her, lifted her from the rock on to which she had climbed and set her firmly on the sand.

'That poor bird – it's hurt!'

'I can see that, and I can get hold of it without having an eye pecked out.' All the same Eduard got his wrist gashed as he caught and subdued the gull, which cried like a cat as he carried it to the jingle.

'We'll take it home and Medevil will set the wing. He knows all about wild things ... we once carried an injured pelican on board the *Pandora*. And another time a baby elephant, which hurt its trunk and had to wear a large bandage on it.'

He held the gull securely, and Ruan took the reins of the pony and drove the jingle home to the chateau. Yseult wanted to hear more about the elephant, a gift from a Thai merchant which they had to give to a zoo when it grew too cumbersome to remain a permanent member of the *Pandora's* crew. 'A pity, that,' Eduard smiled. 'He was a great help when it came to unloading cargo.'

As soon as they reached home Medevil took charge of the gull, and Ruan suggested that she attend to the gash on Eduard's wrist. It was quite deep and could turn nasty, having come from a wild bird.

'There's a first-aid kit in my studio,' he said, and she walked ahead of him up the winding stairs. Yseult had gone off with Medevil to watch the more interesting operation. The studio was dusky in the late afternoon light and Eduard switched on a lamp and took the kit from a cupboard. He sat on the high stool which he used for his bench modelling, and Ruan was intensely conscious of him as she held his wrist and cleaned the cut with antiseptic. He made no murmur, though it must have stung, and for some odd reason she was the one who winced. She glanced up at him, and he quirked his lip in the lopsided smile she was never quite sure of.

'You have a cool and compassionate touch,' he murmured. 'Have you ever thought of becoming a nurse?'

'Hugh asked me the same thing.' She applied antiseptic plaster to the cut and pressed it gently in place, the strip of pink looking delicate against his sun-weathered skin. 'Do you think I ought to go in for a career? Maybe nursing might be the answer when this holiday is over and I return to London. Perhaps I could train at the hospital where Hugh operates. I have the feeling he'd like me to—'

'Are you fond of him? Girls are said to be susceptible to medical men.'

'As sailors are to mermaids?' She was smiling, and then

175

her breath caught in her throat as Eduard closed his hands about her waist and pulled her against him. His face looked hard, his eyes were glinting, and a stray lock of hair on his forehead added to his air of recklessness.

'Shall I thank you in the traditional way, Ruan?' His voice was dangerously soft. 'With a kiss after comfort?'

CHAPTER TEN

HER heart was pounding as she tried to pull away from him, but his hold was too strong to break. She was like a willow caught by the wind ... like foam tossed on a wave ... drowning in the sea-blue eyes as he bent to her and his lips caressed her neck to her earlobe, and took from her lips her whisper of protest.

The tang of the sea was on his lips, and she seemed to hear the lash and roar of the tide. In the storm that was his kiss, she was helpless to do anything but submit to him, and when it was over she was as shocked as a Victorian miss kissed against her will. Her reaction was equal to her sense of outrage – she struck at him with her fist and caught him a blow across the cheek.

He laughed ... laughed and held her, his hair tousled on his brow, his eyes shimmering a flamy blue behind his smoky lashes.

'Who are you trying to punish, me or yourself?' he taunted.

'I hate you!'

'What, for waking you out of the dream into which you fell when Powers touched you? Did you really think his kisses so unique that you'd never respond to any other man – even to me?'

'You forced that kiss upon me!'

'And you liked it! You don't yet know yourself, Ruan Perry, let alone what makes a man. You don't want someone who bends the knee being gallant and tragic. You won't admit it, but the kiss taken is sometimes a lot sweeter than the kiss given. Who wants it to be tame and gift-wrapped? No real woman, and certainly no man with a bit of vitality in him.'

'No!' she flung back at him. 'What you want is a plaything. You're used to girls who think of love as a mere dalliance, like plucking a papaya from a tree, or taking a swim in a lagoon, but this isn't a tropical island and I'm not a papaya girl!'

He gave her that sardonic half-smile of his. 'You've got me all figured out, haven't you? The sea-rover who for the past fifteen years has lived and loved wherever his fancy took him. In some respects you are right, but in all my years of travelling I never left a broken heart behind me when I sailed away on the *Pandora*. Being no saint, I yet have not been quite a satyr.'

He let her go and walked over to the table on which he kept a few decanters and glasses. A glass stopper clinked in the ensuing quiet, and then she saw, through the moist mist of half-strange tears, that he was pouring wine into a couple of the glasses. He returned to her side, his fingers looped about the stems. 'This will settle your shaken nerves,' he said mockingly. 'I guess it isn't every day that you get kissed so thoroughly by a man you can't stand.'

'Wine – in the afternoon?'

'There's no set time for any sort of pleasure, Ruan.' He held out one of the glasses in which the wine had a ruby tint. 'I'm a Talgarth, remember. My grandmother used to drink champagne at breakfast.'

'I believe you take after her.'

'Do you?' His smile was enigmatical. 'Because she pleased herself and did as she fancied all her life?'

'You know what you want and you set out to possess it – as you repossessed the chateau and old treasures belonging to your family.'

'I'm an obstinate man, but I know there is a limit to what I can claim and what I can win.' As he spoke he handed her one of the glasses, and the stem was warm from his touch. 'There's a dream I have, but being a Celt I know that certain things are in the hands of destiny and I can't force her hand.'

'You told me that dreams were not as satisfying as realities.'

'They aren't, Ruan, if they have to remain dreams.' He

drank some of his wine. 'Perhaps you and I are doomed to it, tied to the mast of a dream ship we can never bring to harbour. I want to reach out for what I long for, but for the first time in my life I'm afraid. I think I would sooner keep half my dream than lose all of it, and I wouldn't have made such a compromise when I was younger. I'd have said "to the devil" and taken what I wanted. Tomorrow wouldn't have mattered to me.'

'Because you had the *Pandora* to sail away on?'

'I still have the *Pandora*. I may still sail away, taking but half a dream as my cargo.'

He tossed back his wine and brooded over the Persian puzzle that lay on his work bench, moving with lean fingers the ivory and ebony squares. 'Life is composed of lights and shades; of a daytime and a night-time. We can't snatch daylight out of the night sky, we can only wait for the dawn and hope it will be a shining one.'

He swung his glance to meet hers. 'Laugh, Ruan! You have heard Talgarth being sentimental and profound.'

But she didn't feel like laughing. Cradling her wine glass, she walked to a window that overlooked the sea, where the sun had faded away and misty violet shadows were creeping inland to enfold the chateau. How lonely it must be in the wintertime, and how cold then the sea for a man from the tropics.

She glanced at him as he removed the damp muslin from the half-finished figure of Undine. He met her wondering eyes. 'Would you like to pose for half an hour? I might as well try and get this finished before the roof of the cottage is mended and you return to Pencarne.'

'I – I'm not in costume.'

'You'll do as you are ... please sit for me on that leather hassock.'

She took the pose that now came naturally to her, her profile outlined by the flow of her hair, a waiting look about the slim line of her body. It helped her to sustain the pose if she allowed her thoughts to wander, and upon this occasion they wandered to Avendon, to her stepsister Charme, who had beauty but was hardly the fragile figure of a man's dream. If Eduard had really wanted her, he could so easily have taken her away from Simon Fox ... but he hadn't bothered.

'He just wants someone to share the chateau with him,' Charme had said. 'Anyone will do ... even you, Ruan.'

Charme for once had been wrong about a man. Eduard was in love with a woman and uncertain of her. If he couldn't have her, he meant to sail away on the *Pandora*. Who was she, this dream girl he dared not treat lightly?

'All right, Galatea,' his voice seemed to come from a distance, 'you can relax now and go and get your dinner.'

She gave a little shiver and realized she was cold. Her left foot was numb as she stood up, and a sudden gust of wind launched itself against the walls and windows of the tower.

'It sounds as if a blow is getting up.' He veiled Undine in her clinging muslin and left her like a ghost in the studio. Lower down on the gallery they could hear the waves battering the cliffs, and from a window they saw the intermittent flash of the lighthouse that stood some miles beyond the long curve of the bay. A lonely sentinel guiding the ships past the rocks.

'What does it feel like,' Ruan asked, 'to be on a ship with a tempest blowing?'

'Frightening, but with an edge of excitement to it that makes one realize how good it is to be alive when the danger is past. The *Pandora* once rode out a typhoon that left her battered and becalmed off a small island I mapped and would like to revisit, some day. It was as if we had to go through those hours of hell in order to find that small paradise. If we'd seen it on an ordinary tropical morning, we'd have probably sailed past and forgotten it.'

'Then you believe that only in danger, or grief, or from being hurt, that we come alive to the wonder of being alive?'

'You have it in a nutshell, Ruan. How can there be a great love, for instance, unless we've known a lesser love? One that seemed to offer heaven while it lasted, but gave only a glimpse of the real thing. You can't be a ship's captain until you've been a sailor. You can't fall completely in love until you've fallen half-way.'

She looked at him, compelled by his eyes, drawn into them. 'What are you saying – ?'

'You know very well what I'm saying.'

She knew, and she didn't want to hear any more, she didn't wait to listen, and upon reaching her room she closed the door hastily behind her, as if to shut him out. But he hadn't pursued her. Only his words had done so, and they wouldn't be silenced as the wind grew rougher and the waves sounded as if they were clawing their way to the chateau.

The gale increased in force as Ruan and Yseult ate dinner together. Eduard didn't join them, and Jancey looked curiously grim as she served their pudding. They lingered awhile in the *salon*, but each gust of wind shook the windows and made them jumpy. 'Let's go to bed,' said Ruan, and they fled across the hall like a pair of half-frightened children. The door of Eduard's study was firmly closed, and there was no sign of Medevil. A clock chimed. It was half-past ten, and not a night to be on the moors, or the sea.

Ruan was sleeping restlessly when long wails of distress awoke her. She sat up sharply and realized that they were coming from outside in the gale-lashed night. Someone flung open her door. 'Ruan, are you awake?' Yseult stood breathlessly in the doorway. 'I went down to find out what that fearful noise was, and Jancey told me a ship had gone on the rocks. Eduard and Medevil have gone off to help. Isn't it awful! People might be drowned!'

Ruan got quickly out of bed and began to fling on her clothes. Yseult switched on the lamp and stared at her. 'You look as though you've been crying,' she said.

'Let's go down. Those sirens sound close by and it's more than likely rescued passengers will be brought here to the chateau and we'll help Jancey make sandwiches and beds.'

These words acted like a spur and the next instant the two girls were racing downstairs to take their orders from Jancey, who was calm and practical and as a fisherman's daughter accustomed to these sudden disasters. When the seas were rough, she said, a ship could be swept into trouble in a matter of minutes, but the men of the lifeboat team would do their utmost and there would be few casualties if those Cornish lads had their way.

By midnight Yseult had fallen asleep, worn out on the sofa in the *salon*, but Ruan and Jancey were still busy in the kitchen, where a large pan of soup was simmering, along with pots of coffee. The table was loaded with meat and egg sandwiches, and as many beds as possible had been made up in readiness.

It wouldn't be long now before passengers off the ship began to straggle up the cliffs to the lighted comfort of the chateau. A couple of men had been up from the shore to say that the ship was a privately owned vessel from America, which had been heading for port when she had got herself snarled up on the rocks off St. Avrell. There was damage to her side and she was listing, but the lifeboat had now taken off her passengers and was heading back with them. The lifeboat would then return to the ship to take off the crew.

Ruan and Jancey exchanged a grave look, for in another hour or so the damaged ship would be half under water and it would be a dangerous task to land her crew. 'Have a mug of tea, lass.' Ruan took it gratefully and stood by the great fire drinking it, nervously alert, and trying not to let her imagination picture the high waves sweeping over the sloping decks of the ship, her sea-wet passengers now huddled together on the rescue boat that had to make its way around the cruel rocks to reach the shore, and safety.

They arrived half an hour later, a cold, shivering bunch of people, clutching a few belongings and weeping a little after their ordeal.

As they were ushered into the great warm kitchen, Ruan was ready with coffee, blankets, and a warm word of comfort. There was a couple of children whom she quickly stripped, towelled down, and tucked into a bed comfy with hot-water bottles. She fed them with onion soup and left them sound asleep, returning at once to the kitchen where a refreshed Yseult was handing out food and asking eager questions.

Everyone was eager to talk now they were safe on dry land and under the strong roof of the chateau. Ruan heard all they were saying in a kind of dream, in which she didn't cease for a moment to offer hand and heart to their troubles. One woman had lost her pearls; another was deeply concerned for a fellow passenger who had stayed with the crew for fear of overloading the rescue boat.

'He just wouldn't leave that sinking ship, honey. He said he'd wait for the return of the lifeboat, and that he was sure the good Lord would see to it that everyone was saved.'

'He sounds very brave,' said Ruan, folding a blanket closely about the woman's shoulders. 'Would you like another cup of coffee, or a rum toddy?'

'Coffee, my dear.' A ringed hand caught at Ruan's. 'You Britishers come right out of your shells when other folks have got trouble, don't you? That boy on the ship . . . he's English and the most charming creature. If anything happens to him, I shall be cut to the heart. Why, if I were thirty years younger—'

She winked, but had dozed off in her armchair before Ruan could pour out her coffee.

By half-past two the rescued people had been bedded down for the night, and the kitchen had grown quiet, with an air of waiting. Yseult yawned on a stool in front of the fire, but couldn't be persuaded to go to her own bed. 'I must wait up,' she said drowsily. 'I must see Eduard and be sure he's all right.'

'Mr. Eduard will be right as ninepence,' said Jancey. 'He's a seaman all through, and it's my belief that he pines to be back behind the helm. He's a Talgarth from the old days, when the men of this family were as rugged as my own two brothers, both of whom were out with their boat when the soldiers were brought off the beaches at Dunkirk. What a sight that was, to see the hundreds of little boats returning at dawn with those poor tired lads. We wept and we cheered – ah, I'm getting old, Miss Ruan, and I dwell on my memories, but it's good to have them, if a bit sad.'

Ruan listened to the wind and the pounding of the seas, and tonight her own memories seemed extra poignant. She gave a nervous start as the clock chimed and she counted the three strokes. The tide would be high and the lifeboat would have a struggle to bring those men ashore. Oh God, let them be safe, she prayed. Captain and crew, the lifeboat team, and that man who stayed with the sailors.

The wind had fallen and the first pale shadows of dawn were patching the sky when the sound of voices broke on the stillness ... male voices, hearty with relief, some of them laughing, and yet with a weariness underneath.

A few minutes more and the kitchen was humming with activity and redolent of wet clothing, the smell of the sea, and hot rum toddy. All was bustle and confusion as tall men clustered around the fire and took great bites out of man-sized sandwiches and gulped down the warming soup and coffee and hot sweet tea.

Ruan handed out blankets and searched the flock of men for Talgarth himself. He wasn't to be seen, but over by the door one of the rescued men caught her eye and she gave a strangled little cry of recognition. He was lifting a coffee mug to his lips and he saw her at exactly the same moment.

'Ruan!'

'Tarquin!'

She couldn't believe in the reality of him until she had

pushed through the crowd of men and was actually touching his arm, and then clutching his hand. 'It was you!' she gasped. 'You stayed on board with the crew!'

'Yes,' he laughed. 'Ruan, this is unbelievable. You are real?'

'Of course.' He was the Tarquin of their very first meeting, his grey eyes brilliant in his handsome face, aware of her, remembering all and every moment of their friendship, up until the time the lightning had struck her from his memory for painful weeks. 'You recognize me,' she exclaimed.

'From the moment I saw you, a nymph among all those tousled sailors.'

'You didn't know me, Tarquin, after your accident at the theatre.'

'That was the strangest thing, but just now it all flashed back to me. Ruan – dear nymph.'

'I'm so glad you're all right, and safe. It must have been awful, down there in the water. Tarquin, I'll get you a blanket—'

'No,' he caught and held her back. 'I had a sou'wester and I'm not too wet at all. Stay a moment more. Tell me what you're doing here – this is the house of Eduard Talgarth.'

'Yes – he was with the lifeboat crew. Did you see him?'

'Yes. Big dark chap doing the work of three men getting us off that tipsy ship. She had keeled right over when the Captain left her. I expect Talgarth is with Captain Lake right now. There were coastguards down on the beach, and several officials, and he seems himself to be the nabob of St. Avrell.'

She smiled a little. 'He's just Talgarth, and other people seem to lean on his strength and all that he knows about sea craft. I – I'm glad he's all right.'

'You haven't told me what you're doing here in Cornwall.'

'I'm holiday companion to Yseult – she's over there ladling out soup for that young sailor. Tarquin,' her eyes searched his, 'I heard you had gone to America. Mr. Strathern told Eduard—'

'Eduard?' he said whimsically. 'You were looking very pale and tense until I told you he was safe. You used not to like the man. He was your stepsister's beau, wasn't he?'

'No.' She was shaken by her own emphatic denial. 'She was only a distraction – just as I was.'

'You, Ruan?'

'Yes,' and she could even smile as she added, 'for you.'

'That isn't true,' he protested. 'We found so many things we both liked. Whenever we met it was like a holiday. Whenever we kissed it was as if the sun came out.'

'But love is a storm,' she heard herself saying, 'not just half a day's sunshine. Love is knowing that roses fade as well as bloom, and I think we wanted no more than those sunny hours on the river. We never looked beyond them.'

'We couldn't, not at that time.'

She looked into his eyes and saw a sadness steal into them. She guessed, then, why he had returned from America.

He nodded. 'My wife died very quietly, and it was a release for both of us. She could never have got well.'

'I'm so sorry, Tarquin.'

'But, Ruan, we can go to Rome. I asked you once before and you said you'd come and keep me company.'

'A holiday companion?' Her smile was curiously mature in that moment, and she saw beyond the attraction he had had for her at Avendon and beyond the lonely girl she had been at that time. He was so handsome, but now she knew that the prince had kissed her only half awake.

'You must be hungry,' she said. 'I'll tell Jancey you'd like some soup, or sandwiches.'

'Ruan—'

But she had turned away, and when she reached Jancey at the table she said to her: 'That nice-looking man by the door would like something to eat – I'm taking a flask of soup down to the shore. Mr. Talgarth is there and he'll be cold and famished.'

Jancey gave her such a warm look. 'I was that worried about him and was about to ask someone to take him a bite of food and something to drink. There's some cold fowl in the larder, Miss Ruan.'

'Put it between bread and add some pickles.' They smiled like conspirators. 'I'll go and put my raincoat on.'

'Yes, wrap up. It's a drear morning and misty it'll be down on the shore.'

The gale of the night had died right away, but the dawn had brought mist with it and through the haze the wailing of the seabirds had a desolate sound. Ruan's raspberry-red coat was a splash of colour on the path leading down to the shore, and the trees were rather like ghosts.

There was an oak tree at the bend of the path, where on a bright morning it was good to stand and take in the sea view. Ruan had just reached the tree when something moved, and she gave a startled little cry. A tall figure emerged from the other side of the ancient trunk, a shiny sou'wester dispelling the illusion that he was a spirit of the dawn.

They stood looking at one another, with the tails of mist twining around them. The mist was on his hair and it was unruly and very black. Beads of moisture clung to his cheekbones, and his eyes were intensely blue, like chinks of sky peeping through the early morning haze.

When he didn't speak, she held up the basket of chicken sandwiches and flask of hot coffee. She had decided that he would welcome a cup of coffee. 'I brought you something to take away the chills.'

'You brought yourself,' he said, in that voice that went dangerously soft whenever he spoke to her alone. 'I thought you'd be cosily chatting about old times with a certain friend of yours. Quite a surprise – for both of us – that he was aboard the *Florina*.'

'Has she gone right down, Eduard?'

'Yes. Nice little craft as well, but the rocks of St. Avrell

187

are dangerous and they bit her in the side. She slowly flooded.'

'It was a miracle that her passengers and crew were saved.'

'A miracle for you, Ruan?'

'For me?'

'Tarquin Powers was among them.'

'I know.' She approached him under the tree. 'Shall I pour you a cup of coffee? It's strong and sweet, the way you like it.'

'You're being very nice to me,' he said whimsically. 'Grateful that I helped save your boy-friend?'

'Don't—'

'You're always saying don't to me. What did you say to him?'

'That I was so glad he was all right – *Eduard!*' She cried out and dropped the food basket as strong, hurting hands took hold of her and crushed her against the oak tree, a prisoner in a red raincoat, her misty hair clinging like autumn leaves around her temples and her slender neck. 'Eduard—'

'So it's glad you are that he's safe and well, and when, may I ask, do the pair of you leave for Rome? I take it his memory is restored and you'll take up where you left off?'

'If you don't leave off bullying me—' Suddenly the strain of the night was taking its toll and tears filled Ruan's eyes. 'I was so worried – all night – even when there was so much to do – and now you're being mocking and cruel.'

'Worried – about me?'

'Yes, is it so hard to believe?'

'You'd worry about a fly on the hob.' And then he fell silent and his blue eyes were roving her face, taking in each contour, each feature, especially the tears that crept down her cheeks until one of them disappeared inside her dimple. 'You odd child, laughing and crying, and down here with me instead of up there with Powers.'

'Yes, isn't it crazy? Why do I bother to bring you coffee when he's so handsome and gallant – and no longer a married man?'

'Is that a fact?' Eduard's eyes narrowed dangerously. 'Well, it looks as if you'll be taking him coffee from now on. I suppose this morning is just a bit of good will, because I helped to save him for you?'

'Brute!'

'Do you think he'd miss a kiss from the bride-to-be? All heroes get kissed.'

'Devil!'

He laughed—laughed and held her, there beneath the great misty canopy of the oak tree, and when he kissed her it wasn't anything but stormy heaven. All she felt was the touch of his lips on hers, warm and vital and tangy from the sea. She forgot everything else, even the dream girl about whom he had spoken in his studio last night.

'Ruan,' it was like the surf murmuring her name, 'you'd better not tell Powers about that kiss.'

'I never shall,' she murmured. 'He'll be leaving the chateau quite early, I think. I expect he has to be in Rome quite soon.'

'Where you'll be joining him?'

'No. I shall be here in Cornwall, companion to Yseult, model for Undine.' She drew back a little and looked into Eduard's blue eyes. 'Who is she, the girl you can't have, who might send you sailing away with half a dream as cargo? I feel I'd like to know.'

'Maybe you have a right to know.' He stroked from her wondering eyes a russet strand of hair. 'She's quite a bit younger than the leathery sinner who loves her. She has a heart that shines in her eyes, and a mouth that's like a rose to kiss. She has a tender spirit, and also a fighting one, and the second time I saw her I came close to carrying her off with me to my lonely chateau. I don't know why I didn't, but at that time she couldn't see the moon for the stars in her eyes, and I wanted her to love me.'

He paused, and then said softly, 'If she couldn't love me of her own free will, then the *Pandora* was always ready and waiting. If you can't love me, Ruan, I'll sail away with half a dream.'

'Me?' she whispered.

'Yes, from the moment you gave me the cold shoulder in the foyer of the Mask Theatre, all eagerness to get to your seat to see the entrance of your princely actor.'

'But you came to Avendon to see my stepsister.'

'I came to see a girl called Ruan. St. Cyr talked about you, and I was intrigued by your name and I wondered if it could belong to a girl equally rare and lovely. Ruan,' a smile slashed his brown cheek, 'as a Celt you're supposed to have second sight. Couldn't you tell that I cared?'

'You were never as kind to me as you are to Yseult.'

'Yseult is a child, and a man isn't kind to the woman he loves — he's so full of wanting that he can't be anything but a little cruel. If you only knew, Ruan. If you only cared—'

'I do care!'

The world was blue in an instant, no clouds, no mist, no harsh waves pounding the shore. A ray of sun broke through from the east, and the birds began to wheel about with cheerful cries.

'This morning when I saw Tarquin it made me happy to see he was safe and well — but it made me come alive all through my body to hear that you were unhurt. Eduard, it isn't possible to love greatly until we have loved romantically. Tarquin was my romance ... you are my love.'

His eyes were brilliant when she revealed at last what he had waited to hear. With a vibrant tenderness he enfolded her in his arms, and her hair blew against his cheek as they stood together and watched the sun arise. The day would be a shining one, and the years ahead for both of them would be lonely no more.

'Eduard,' she murmured, 'your coffee will get cold.'

Take these 4 best-selling novels FREE

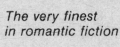 

Harlequin Presents...

The very finest in romantic fiction

Get all the latest books before they're sold out!
As a Harlequin subscriber you actually receive your personal copies of the latest Presents novels immediately after they come off the press, so you're sure of getting all 6 each month.

Cancel your subscription whenever you wish!
You don't have to buy any minimum number of books. Whenever you decide to stop your subscription just let us know and we'll cancel all further shipments.

Your FREE gift includes

Sweet Revenge by **Anne Mather**
Devil in a Silver Room by **Violet Winspear**
Gates of Steel by **Anne Hampson**
No Quarter Asked by **Janet Dailey**